•••

THE
APPLE

•••

•••

THE
APPLE

•••

A NOVEL BASED ON
THE HERMAN ROSENBLAT HOLOCAUST
LOVE STORY

By
Penelope J. Holt

York House Press, Ryebrook, NY

York House Press
800 Westchester Avenue, Suite 641 North
Ryebrook, NY 10573

ISBN 13: 978-0-9791956-4-8, York House Press
First edition, September 2009
Library of Congress number in progress

Cover design by Concise Marketing & Communications

Printed in the United States of America

For all the children lost to genocide,

our hearts have broken for you.

Author's Note

The Holocaust is perhaps the best-researched and documented event of the 20th century. It cannot be denied, at least not by rational people. Neither can it be denied that Herman Rosenblat spent from 1939-1945 in ghettos and Nazi concentration and slave labor camps. He suffered and emerged with an authentic survivor or shoah account. And finally, it cannot be denied that Herman did fabricate key aspects of his account. Everyone seems to agree on all of these things. What they can't seem to agree on are the reasons why Herman embellished his story. Explanations run the gamut; some people are understanding of Herman and his motivations, others remain critical. I leave readers to make up their own minds.

This novel tells Herman's story and also the story behind the story— what happened after his account became public and created a perfect pop-culture storm, complete with gotcha journalism, adventures in culture making, publishing dilemmas, modern victimhood, sacred cows, freedom of speech and storytelling, new media and the power of the Internet to explode a story.

Some characters in the book have retained their real names, while the names of others have been changed. Much of the novel is based on real events in Herman's life, although certain incidents are fictionalized. I have also woven in other authentic individual or composite accounts from survivors who were in the same places, at the same time as Herman, during the war. I am particularly grateful for two sources: *The Buchenwald Report* as translated by David A. Hackett, 1995, Westview Press, and *The Boys* by Martin Gilbert, Henry Holt and Company, 1997. Make no mistake, the conditions, events, and SS behavior I describe in Piotrkow, Buchenwald, Schlieben and Theresienstadt were real and experienced either by Herman or by others who were in those places at that time.

Holocaust survivors are remarkable people. The children of the Holocaust, like Herman, are in their seventies and eighties now and dwindling in number. We have their accounts, but sadly, we are losing the flesh and blood of them. I have learned that these people are altered by their experiences in ways that the rest of us cannot conceive. Because of the hell that they lived through and carried with them afterwards, I believe that they walk on a different stratum of human experience than the rest of us. I feel privileged to have spent time with a survivor, with Herman. I feel changed by it, for the better. Woken up and shaken up.

The Holocaust historians and survivors who brought Herman's embellishments to light have my respect and admiration as they guard and protect the truth. It is not my place to apologize for Herman and the hurt that his behavior may have caused. But, maybe because I am the mother of a thirteen year old boy, the age that Herman was when his mother was sent away to be gassed in Treblinka, it is my hope that the Holocaust and the collective community can seek to understand and forgive the individual survivor and his story.

Penelope Holt, Pound Ridge, April 2009

Acknowledgements

Thanks to my husband, Richard, for sanity and strength. My children and my family—all of them, for purpose and belonging. My trusted reader, Lisa. My cheerleader, Val. My mentor, Bob. My publishing partners. Laurie, who helps make good things happen. Herman, for his strong survivor spirit and love of life. Harris, who is a determined storyteller. Peter Kubicek, who disagreed without being disagreeable. The Holocaust survivors and historians whose accounts enriched my understanding and troubled my heart.

THE APPLE

Chapter One
The Apple

Somewhere up there is a devil with a rifle at the ready and he will shoot anyone who comes near the fence. The boy stares at the frozen raindrops glistening on the icy necklace of barbed wire. He waits and hunches over as the cold knifes him, shrinking further into the flapping tissue of his blue and white striped pajamas. In the dawn light, he is so thin he might disappear; undersized for 15 and emaciated. He thinks about his mother and whispers her name--Mamusia, hugging himself tight until he can finger both boney shoulder blades. It's been forever since he was warm. Scanning the snowy tree line beyond the fence, he mouths her name again--Mamusia.

Snow slides off a branch and he sees the girl step out from between two trees. He glances up at the watchtower and a jolt of fear hits him. The girl picks a path through the snow and crunches towards him. He can see that she is thin too, but she looks sturdy in woolen stockings, a heavy jacket and a beret; a slash of bright blue dress shows below her coat. She stops and looks at him through the taught wire and barbs. The boy drops his shoulders as a smile lifts the girl's mouth and crinkles her brown eyes. He sees her small white teeth.

She reaches in her pocket and pulls out an apple like a magician presenting a conjured object. Now he smiles. The apple is more than nourishment. It is warmth and relief from fear that has devoured so much that now fear is almost all of him. The girl pushes her palm forward. Watching? Gracefully, she tosses the apple. It rises in an arc through clear, cold air, like a small comet trailing a tail of light with just enough force to graze the fence top. The boy watches the girl lift her beautiful face--wide cheekbones and dark almond eyes. Her chin tilts up as she tracks the apple's ascent. He cups his hands and waits, his eyes fixed, not on the apple, but on the angel beyond the fence. A few more seconds and the golden round will land in the well made by his battered, raw, boney hands with their chipped and filthy nails, and swollen fingers. Hands for a man of 80, not a boy of 15.

"Herman, wake up." Herman opened his eyes and looked into his wife's deep brown ones. She was leaning over him as he dozed in an easy chair in the warm rays of a Florida sun. "Someone on the phone for you." Roma frowned. More unwelcome intrusions. Herman stood, gave his head a small shake and took the cordless.

"Herman, this is Colin, a producer at the Oprah Show." The voice was unfamiliar but Herman thought he remembered the name. He was the young TV guy. One of the staff who had helped Roma and him when they appeared on Oprah last February. The Valentine's Day show about inspiring love stories.

"Herman," Colin ventured, "Oprah would like you to come back on the show to explain your side of the story."

"My family does not want me to go on the show. They don't want me talking to no press." After 60 years, Herman still carried a thick Polish accent, but he dropped the finer points of English that he had learned after the war, when he ditched Polish, the language of his suffering. "There is a lot of anger and negativity right now. A lot of people are attacking me. They don't understand."

"Oprah does not want to attack you, Herman. She just wants you to answer the allegations and tell your side of the story. Clear the whole thing up. Don't you want to set the record straight?" Colin was reassuring.

"I do but I can't. Tell Oprah that I am sorry about everything. I do want to explain, but the family doesn't want me to do it." Herman felt the bind he was in. He was too nervous to back out of the promise he had made to his family--to stay quiet until the storm blew itself out. "The family lawyer has told me not to do it," he told Colin now. "Maybe when people are not so angry."

"Herman, call me if you change your mind." The producer gave it one last try.

"I will. Thank you. Goodbye." Herman rushed the goodbye and hung up.

He dropped back in his chair, shifting about, bubbling with un-ease, a helplessness he had not felt in over 65 years. As a child in the camps of Buchenwald and Schlieben, it had been a fact of his life as a Jew that it did no good to explain how you suffered or to ask for understanding. Why make a case for survival to SS? They were so sure that no Jew, not even a Jewish child, had the right to exist.

Of course this mish gosh over his book was not so serious, he thought. No one is trying to kill me. But there was hate mail, from the usual anti-Semites. They were always around to police the world against Jews. Herman read their letters, the emails and blogs. Same message: die, Jew, die. Of course, what else? But other Jews attacking him too? One letter last week that...No, no, forget it. Why dwell on bad things?

He was getting calls from the press like the one just now from Oprah. They said that they wanted to give him a chance to explain himself, but he caught the danger in their invitations. He heard it--

that strained note. People claimed that they were sympathetic, but underneath, they seemed ready to pounce. Herman had spent his childhood in a sound garden of terrifying noises, cruel voices with not a single note of mercy in them. He knew the sound of closed, critical minds and deaf, unwilling ears and he heard its murmur now.

Herman went over the problem again. The problem of his book. I am a survivor. I know about suffering, he thought. The book was supposed to be a message of hope that made people feel better. Instead people were getting mad and disgusted. No not everybody. Plenty of people support me. But the critics are angry and they make the most noise. What a mess. He couldn't unravel it. Yes I made a mistake. I have to put it right. I know. But when? Not right now. Herman felt undone by all the hostility and not sure what to do next. He was mute, like in a dream when you try to speak but no words come out. Maybe later, he thought. When people can listen without getting mad. Maybe then, I'll have a chance to say I'm sorry. I'm sorry I disappointed you.

Herman looked out the window at a far-off strip of water. He wondered again why he had gone into the room where he had sealed off all thoughts of the Holocaust. Why had he unlocked the door, broken the seal, and turned on the light of memory? He had been like all the other survivors he knew after the war. He had closed down the past and shut it out. Locked the door and turned off the light. The nightmare was over. Why think of it again? He had a chance for a new life. Don't squander a precious future dwelling on past agony, he told himself. And, for years, it was easy to stay quiet about what had happened when he was a child, a Polish Jew in German concentration camps. To forget about 1939 to 1945. Scrub those years out. But then came a fall morning in 1992 and the second greatest catastrophe of Herman Rosenblat's life.

Herman riffled through his memories. He found the day: November 18th, back when he still had the electrical business in Brooklyn--Rosenblat Electrical Company. The offices were in the small three-storey brick building he owned. It was early, 7:20 AM. He knew the time because he had glanced at the clock right before all the chaos erupted. He and Kenneth had been there, the only ones at the office. Herman was happy that morning, he remembered. It was the kind of day when small but satisfying plans come together. Life felt good. Business was doing pretty well. He was planning a company Thanksgiving party for the next day and he was sweetening his workers' wages with bonuses. A lot to be thankful for. Herman had been thinking just this when he heard an outside door open then close. Who came in? It was the wrong sound at the wrong time. No employees were due yet. It was too early.

"I'll get it," Kenneth said, standing up and ambling out to the hall. Herman heard a gunshot, turned, and saw his son fall in the narrow hallway. The intruder burst into the office. His fast eyes scanned the room and clicked on the money stacked on Herman's desk. He lunged for it, but reflexively, Herman had already grabbed for the pile. A popping sound. A burning sensation in his gut. Herman peered down at his white shirt and touched his belly. Wet? Blood seeping out? His attacker was gone, but Herman could not stand upright; he was swaying. The phone was there, just out of reach. He groped for it, scraped the green receiver towards him and dialed 911. "We've been shot. My son and me. We've been shot and we've been robbed," he croaked into the mouthpiece and then he fell.

He eyed Ken in the hallway but didn't think he could get there. Crawling across an acre of linoleum, he finally reached his son.

"How are you?" Herman asked but he couldn't see where Ken was shot or how badly he was hurt. Oh God, please don't let him die. "I can't feel my legs," Ken moaned. Herman curled up close to him, both of them inert, propelled by the force of the attacker's bullets into the sudden crisis of a dark new reality.

Now time stopped as they waited for help, but Herman was not sure it would come. In shock from his gunshot wound, he hovered around consciousness. He heard the sound of ambulances, far away at first and then so close that the sirens were penetrating his brain. People leaned over him. They were unexpected; uninvited visitors to his world. Alien speech crackling on a police walkie-talkie. A patch of darkness. Noise and movement. Herman was flat out on a stretcher, tucked under a blanket, like a child ready for bed. Bright lights in a distant ceiling. Riding a gurney. Gliding fast and smooth. He was wheeled down corridors and around the sharp angle of hospital corners, the smell of wet floors and disinfectant in his nostrils. He stopped. The gurney was angled into an elevator. Going up. And then pulled out. Was he dying? Hard to know from inside this vortex of controlled activity where he lay totally disconnected and yet at the center of everything. The gurney slowed then stopped. He was in an operating room.

Herman looked up at the distorted face of a doctor who leaned into view and peered down at him over a green surgical mask that covered his mouth and nose. Memories of SS doctors at Buchenwald crowded Herman's mind. They had protected themselves with masks from the stench and disease. They prodded and probed; cavity-searching prisoners for valuables, for gold fillings in mouths full of teeth that were snapped and broken down from starvation, neglect, or the butt of an SS rifle or stick. In a single year, they yanked pounds and pounds of gold fillings. It went to Buchenwald's metal shop. The jewelers and skilled metal workers there shaped it into rings and pocket watches; jewelry for SS peacocks. Officers wore the booty or used it for bribes or to make gifts to superiors. A bow for those above. A boot for those below.

"How is my son? Can he move his legs?" Herman whispered but the doctor ignored him. He motioned to the anesthesiologist. Push the button on the drugs and knock the patient out. Drifting into oblivion, despair snatched at Herman. Dear God, have I survived so much horror for it to end this way?

Hours later, Herman came to in a clean, quiet hospital room. Nothing hurts, he thought, but my mind feels wooly. He closed his eyes and then reopened them. There was his mother, resting lightly on the edge of his bed. That's my favorite black dress, the one with the fine lace collar, he thought. Her dark hair was parted in the middle and pulled back in a bun that rested at the nape of her neck. Her warm serious eyes were watching him. She lifted his hand, it felt heavy and drugged, and she let it rest in her own small two. "Herman, my good boy, I am here," she said. "You know, I want you to tell your story. Tell your story so that your grandchildren will know what happened to their grandfather." She touched his face the way she used to when he was young, palming his cheek; a warm reassuring pressure. Herman closed his eyes so he could be 13 again and savor his mother's loving caress.

He heard the click of a woman's heels on the corridor outside. Roma came in and brought a trace of chill fall air with her. She perched on the edge of the bed right where his mother had sat just a moment ago. Herman did not say hello. "After nearly 50 years," he said instead, and then stopped, surprised that his voice sounded so strong. He started over. "After nearly 50 years of saying nothing, I want to tell my story now."

Chapter Two
Flight

Herman watched his father and mother, his Tatus and Mamusia, as they stood in the street at the entrance of their apartment building in Bydgoszcz. Mamusia had on her best hat, heavy coat, gold-buckled shoes, and she was holding a single silver candlestick. "Jacob, let go," she said. "I want to go back up and get the other one." Herman saw her try to wriggle out from his father's grasp. Tatus looked nervous. "Rose, get in the wagon, everything will be here when we get back," he said, tugging her sleeve, trying to pull her towards the horse and wagon where Sam and Herman were already planted.

Boom. Fireworks in the distance. No, not fireworks, Herman remembered, German artillery. The German army had invaded Poland just days ago. His family had heard the news on the radio. "September 1, 1939 is a day that we will never forget," Tatus had said as they all sat in a tense circle around the kitchen table, leaning in to hear the reports.

Soon, German troops, tanks and heavy equipment began pouring into Poland. And German planes were in the skies. Whenever he heard the drone of approaching aircraft, Herman ran outside into the street and looked up. Tipping back his head and capping his eyes, he followed the path of the planes as they flew over him and then disappeared to a speck in the bright blue sky.

"We have to leave today," Tatus had announced that morning when he came home. He pointed out the window and down onto the street. Herman saw the horse-drawn wagon and driver that his father had hired to take the family to safety in the south. Bydgoszcz was not far from the German border. The German army would make it here in no time, Tatus told the family as he pushed them to finish packing, but he knew better. He knew that German troops were already in the city. He had seen them. Seen the commotion as he hurried home with the wagon and driver. Nazis were in Bydgoszcz, rounding up Jews, dragging them from their homes and businesses into the street, and taking them away.

Now, Herman felt his father's panic, his rush to get out of the city. He wished his big brothers were home. But Isydor was 28 and Abraham was 26, more than old enough to fight, so they had gone off to join the Polish army. They were going to thrash the Germans and then come home. Sam was 18 and he had wanted to go too but Isydor had made him stay back. "You have to watch out for the others," Isydor had insisted, but Sam didn't want to. "Herman can stay and be the caretaker," he complained.

"Herman is only 10," Isydor argued. Sam had to stay.

Isydor had instructed Tatus to go south to Wolborz. Father's sister, Aunt Hannah, her husband, Uncle Avram, and their two sons, Barak and Lutek, lived in the town, a 180 miles to the southeast. The Germans would never make it to Wolborz, and when the brave Polish army beat the Nazis back across the border, then everyone would come back home to Bydgoszcz and be together again.

Mamusia finally climbed into the wagon, but Herman saw that she was fretting about Isydor and Abraham and the trip to Wolborz. At least she doesn't have to worry about Eva, he thought. Eva was 22, and safe in France. She went to visit family and wound up staying because she married a nice man, a friend of the family. She brought him home once to meet her family in Poland and then went straight back to France to live with him there. Herman missed her. She was the best sister in the world. She was only supposed to go for a visit, not get married and stay in stupid France forever. He was glad she was safe, but it would be better if she were here.

"Get up." The driver flicked his whip at the horse and the wagon rolled forward. Herman was sandwiched between his parents. He picked up the tension in their bodies. Like a tuning fork struck by their anxious vibrations, he heard the thrum of their racing minds and realized that they were both afraid. For months they had been talking non-stop about what would happen to the Jews in Poland if the Germans came. Father was a tailor and ran his business from their eight-room apartment. Isydor was a dentist and kept a small lab there too. Almost every night, the family would gather around the kitchen table to talk about the same problems: what will happen if Germany invades Poland? What is going to happen to the Jews? Is it true what people are saying that Hitler is rounding up Jews in Germany and sending them to camps? Death camps.

Herman used to sit on the floor listening quietly, with his back to the wall, and his knees pulled up. If the adults noticed him, they usually chased him out; they didn't want him listening to adult conversation. His parents and brothers argued and paced, frowned and worried, but Herman wasn't scared. He watched from his vantage point on the floor. Everything was fine. There was his mother in the kitchen, right in the middle of it all, cooking like always; making the food. Her cooking drew them like a magnet to the family table in the middle of the warm loving home, where they were all together and safe.

Herman watched his parents scan the road. They looked from side to side, peering into alleyways, as they crept out of Bydgoszcz. Now and then, in the distance, he caught a glimpse of soldiers who leapt from green army trucks onto the streets. "Tatus, are they Germans?" he asked his father. "Be quiet," Tatus snapped and then he reached across to take Mamusia's hand and he squeezed it. She was sitting very stiff and looking straight ahead like she was holding her breath and staying very still to prevent their world from changing. Finally, she turned to face Tatus and Herman saw that she was wearing the saddest look on her face. "Oh, Jacob," she whispered, "they are coming to take the Jews away."

One day Herman had overheard Abraham trying to explain the predicament of the Polish Jews to Sam, who was slouched in a chair at the kitchen table with his violin on his lap, a crooked finger softly plucking at a string. Herman saw that Sam really wanted to practice and not have to listen to Abraham spew on about what he had been reading in the papers.

"It really started in 1935," Abraham intoned like he was reading from a book. "That's when Hitler promulgated laws to hurt the Jews called the Nuremberg racial laws. These laws meant that the German government and legal system could punish Jews, strip their rights, and exclude them in every way possible from German life. The laws institutionalized racial hatred."

Sam turned away trying to look as bored as possible. Abraham pivoted slightly so he was facing Herman instead. Herman was just nine and the lecture was too much for him, but now it seemed that he was the only one listening.

"The laws gave Germans carte blanche to step up more bigotry and violence against Jews," Abraham said.

"What's bigotry?" Herman asked.

"When someone hates you just because you are a Jew," Abraham said. "All this gave the Jew haters in Poland an excuse to go after the same kind of laws. That's why all the Jews in Europe became anxious and afraid. Then in 1938, the Polish Government gave Polish Jews living in Germany an ultimatum."

"What's an ultimatum?" Herman said.

"When someone says do what I say or else," Abraham said. "They gave them an ultimatum: come home to Poland or you will lose your passports. That's why so many Polish Jews came home across the border into Bydgoszcz. We know what Hitler is doing now. He is rounding up German Jews, confiscating their property, and sending them to concentration camps where he can kill them."

"What's confiscate?" Herman asked and then he noticed Isydor standing in the doorway. "Abraham, that's enough," Isydor said.

"He wants to know," Abraham replied.

"He doesn't want to know." Isydor was frowning. "Herman go outside and play." Herman got up to leave. Isydor was right. He really didn't want to know. He didn't understand all this talk about Hitler and the Nazis and why it was important to them. Their family was safe. Every week, they enjoyed a nice Shabbat dinner on Friday and a peaceful Shabbat every Saturday. Lots of talking and kidding around and music. Herman was learning the violin, but he couldn't play very well. He held the instrument under his chin, drew the bow, and it only whined. But the other four were amazing. Before Eva went to France, they played together as a beautiful quartet for Mamusia and Tatus who sat in the parlor listening, Mamusia with her eyes closed and swaying a little. Just fantastic. Herman was fit to burst with pride.

There was a word that Herman heard over and over and he knew what it meant: anti-Semite. It meant people who hate Jews. Anti-Semites were the reason his family had left Pruszcz, the town where he was born. He didn't remember it because they had fled when he was still just a baby. Pruszcz was near Gdansk, close to the shore of the Baltic Sea. It was a tiny village, just a small settlement really with one road, a handful of houses, a few stores and a coffee bar, where the farmers gathered to talk and trade.

Herman's parents had run a small general store selling clothes and equipment--supplies that the local farmers needed. Abraham was 16 then and he helped Mamusia with the store because Tatus and Isydor were living 85 miles away in Bydgoszcz. Tatus was running his tailoring business there and Isydor was training to be a dentist. Tatus tried make the trip back to Pruszcz twice a week, and Eva and Sam, who were only 12 and 8 at the time, went to school; they got to ride the train that went back and forth to Bydgoszcz every day. Pruszcz was so small that it didn't even have its own train station. If you wanted to catch a train, you had to run along side it, and hop on when it slowed down.

Abraham told Herman that there was only a handful of Jews in Pruszcz and the Polish Christians didn't like them, "They used to call us dirty Jews and other rotten names," he said. "They stood outside the store telling people not to buy from us, and waving placards that 'Jews Go to Palestine'. Nearly every week, a bunch of them would break the store windows and try to steal our stuff. I'd run out and chase after them to try and take it back, but they used to beat me up. It wore on mother. She got very down, that's why Tatus had to bring us all to live in Bydgoszcz."

Herman was glad because Bydgoszcz was better. It was a big city with about 300,000 people living in it and not as much anti-Semitism, at least not in the beginning. Herman learned to speak

German and Polish because in Bydgoszcz nearly half the people were Poles and the other half were Volkedeutsch, who lived in Poland, but acted like they were still in Germany. They wore traditional German dress and ate German food and spoke German and did just about everything the German way. There were more Jews in Bydgoszcz too, a few hundred Jewish families.

In Bydgoszcz, Herman had a nice life, shopping with his parents, trips to the opera sometimes and ice-skating. At first, anti-Semitism in Bydgoszcz wasn't so bad, but by the time he was seven or so, the people who hated Jews were getting really fired up. Abraham went on about it all the time. Hitler was fanning the flames and inciting Poles to organize more violent demonstrations. They started waving the same placards that they had in Pruszcz: 'Go to Palestine, Dirty Jews'. One evening, Herman and his parents were coming out of the theater. They had just seen a wonderful play about a man who loves two beautiful women and can't decide which one to marry. Out front, there was a mob of angry Germans and Poles demonstrating. Tatus spotted them and did an about face, hustling the family out the back. He was scared, Herman could tell, even though he said not to worry. "It's flaring up now," Tatus said, "but things will calm down."

"It's going to get worse not better," Abraham argued. And he was right, it did get worse and Mamusia got very worried. She wanted Herman where she could see him every second. But Herman still didn't really fret about anti-Semitism, not until it came looking for him when he started school in first grade. On his way to school in the mornings, he used to stand frozen in the street as Christian boys blocked his path, knocked him down, and called him a dirty kike. And spit, sometimes they spit at him.

Herman complained to his father. "Ignore them, they'll stop soon," Tatus said. That's what he said every single time that

Herman complained to him. Tatus was always trying to ignore it, spinning a lot of wishful thinking: pay no attention. Bound to stop soon. This sort of thing always dies out eventually. Mother was a worrier but Tatus was always hoping for the best. Herman hoped for the best too, but no luck. The bullies at school, they never ran out of steam.

One day, Herman devised a new plan. He went to Eva. His sister had babied him ever since he could remember. "Eva," he said, "on the way to school, boys are knocking me down and calling me names. One of them says he will protect me if I pay him ten groszy."

"Then I shall give you ten groszy." Eva smiled. And she kept her word. She pressed the money into Herman's palm every morning as he set out for school so he could pay his minder, but then she had to leave to go to France, so she stuck the job on Abraham. "Make sure you give Herman ten groszy every morning to pay off the bullies," Eva told him and then she kissed Herman on his forehead. "We're not going to let anyone hurt you, baby brother."

Herman coughed up the protection money and most of the kids at school left him alone, but teachers couldn't be bought. One day, the Catholic boys were finishing catechism class, while the Jewish kids killed time outside, playing in the yard. Herman looked up. The priest had flung open an upper window and was shouting down at them: "There they are, the Jews who killed Christ!" The priest jabbed an accusing finger towards Herman and his friends. Herman saw the Christian boys come charging towards them. They knocked him on the ground and punched him. In class, he limped up to the teacher. He pointed to his cut lip and knee. "Please, sir, I'm bleeding. I need to go to the infirmary."

"I don't see any blood," the teacher said. Herman just stood there thunder struck, didn't know what to say. The teacher was a grown up and he was supposed to care about children. How could he be so unkind? At home, Herman put his schoolbag on the hall table and went to find Tatus. "Who is Jesus and why does the priest say that we killed him?"

"Ignore them, Herman," Tatus said. "They just don't like Jews." Tatus turned his palms up like the whole thing was beyond him. But why didn't they like Jews? Herman wrestled his hurt and confusion. The people in his family were very nice, very fine and friendly. Why would anyone hate them and want to punish them?

Life at school went from bad to worse. Classmates spilled ink on his homework and sabotaged his tests to make him fail.

"Herman has not passed his exams and cannot proceed to second grade," the teacher told his father. Tatus was going up all the time to petition for Herman and to complain about the unkind treatment, but his intervention didn't do much good. It took weeks of pleading before the teacher would allow Herman to move up to second grade. Now it was September, and Herman was supposed to be in third grade, but Hitler had invaded Poland, and he had a plan for the Jews that put paid to Herman's education. No more school for Jews.

As their wagon moved away from the outskirts of Bydgoszcz and onto quieter back roads, Herman could feel his parents start to relax a little and that's when he started to get excited. This was his first real trip away from home, his first adventure. Inside the wagon, he huddled under blankets, breathing in the sharp air. The steady clip of the horse's hooves on the icy roads lulled him. Boom. Every now and then the distant shelling started up but Herman managed to filter it out. We're not really in any danger, he thought.

The trip was slow going and excitement soon turned to boredom. The horse could only plod along, covering no more than 30 or so miles each day. And at the end of an exhausting day's travel, when the family stopped at roadside hostelries looking for a room or an evening meal, Polish innkeepers scowled at them and wanted to know if they were Jews. They didn't look particularly Jewish, so Herman learned to shake his head. "No, we're not he Jews," he said.

After five long tedious days, they finally covered the 185 miles from Bydgoszcz to Wolborz. Aunt Hannah and her whole family were waiting on their doorstep to welcome them and Herman couldn't help but stare because they all looked so Jewish. Uncle Avram wore a kippah on his head, a long black coat and a long beard. Aunt Hannah wore a shteitl, a wig that covered her hair at all times. And Barak and Lutek had ear locks that hung down.

The travelers were exhausted, and Herman had just taken his place at the table for Sabbath dinner when Uncle Avram made an announcement. "It's not safe to stay in Wolborz," he said. The Germans will be here in a matter of days. The only place we'll be safe is in Warsaw. Tomorrow is Shabbat so we will have to wait until Sunday and then leave."

Two nights of rest, and come Sunday, they were off again, packing up the wagon and trying to make room for four more passengers. Herman watched his mother squeeze her hairbrush into the carpetbag she had stuffed. She looked up, suddenly brought to attention by the thought of something missing. "Where is Sam?" Everyone was ready to leave but Sam was nowhere to be found. No one had seen him since breakfast. "Sam, where are you? Sam?" Mamusia stood in Uncle Avram's yard, calling for Sam, the restless one, the renegade. It was time to go, but she refused to get in the wagon.

"Please, Rose, get in. Sam will be alright." Tatus took her hand and pulled her towards a seat. Herman patted the place he was saving for her and saw the tears spilling down her cheeks. He understood. It was bad enough that Isydor and Abraham were in harm's way but now Sam had taken off on his own.

"Where has he gone? Why has he done this?" Mamusia pulled her hands up to her face. Herman pushed his head against her coat sleeve. "Don't cry, Mamusia," he said, leaning on her arm. Rose tried to smile. "As long as I have you, Herman, I'll be okay." She took his hand, uncurled his small tense fist, pressed it flat, and then kissed his palm.

Herman was becoming discouraged. No matter what happened out there in the world, no matter how mean and hateful people were to him, he had always felt that it couldn't really hurt him, because every day he came home, back to the apartment where it was safe, where his family was. Even after Eva left and his brothers took off to fight in the war, Herman had still felt confident. They'll be back soon, he thought. They will all come home and we will do everything just like we used to. But now, they had left their home and the family was all broken up and scattered in different places.

The journey began to feel like a dream where you can't outrun the boogey man. The family couldn't get away from the drone of overhead planes and the boom of nearby artillery. The Germans were close, advancing faster than anyone could have guessed. Riding in the wagon, Herman scrutinized his aunt's family again. It was so obvious that they were Jews. There's just no hiding it, he thought. Now, how are we going to get gentiles to sell us a room? Tatus tried to keep them out of sight when he went looking for food and shelter. "Stay here, while we go up the road to bring back something to eat," he said, urging them to hang back. Still, some nights, the best he could do was to scrounge for room in a barn, where the family could at least dry off and collapse until morning.

As the days went by, Herman watched as Uncle Avram refused every meal because it was not kosher. The old man shook his head and held up both palms, objecting to the food that Tatus offered him. Mamusia kept kosher, but Herman could tell that for Uncle Avram and Aunt Hannah the practice meant much more. Right now, his uncle had skipped so many meals that he was starting to look frail. "Please Avram, eat the chicken," Tatus pleaded one day, but Uncle Avram was stubborn. He shook his head. "Just give me the water," he said.

"But the cup is treyf. It's unclean," Tatus argued, pushing the plate of food at his brother-in-law.

Before he saw tears, Herman noticed his uncle's silent weeping. He was shaking, and his shoulders were moving up and down, and Aunt Hannah was crying too. Herman didn't really understand but he could see that eating food not ritually prepared according to their laws was too much for them. Finally, worn out and weak from hunger, the defeated pair gave in. They sat in the wagon on the roadside, eating joyless bites of roast chicken as the tears slid down their faces. Herman looked away. It wasn't right to watch old people cry.

By the time the wagon reached the outskirts of Warsaw, everyone was exhausted. Lulled into a stupor by the cold and monotony, they slumped down in the wagon as the horse clopped down a narrow road, bordered by woods. The morning dragged on and the shelling grew louder. Mortars were exploding closer and more often. Deafening blasts and reverberations jolted the riders and kept them on edge. Herman could hear the fighting; it was just up the road to the west. In his seat, he pushed his body forward in a rhythmic thrust. Go faster, go faster, he was willing the horse and driver to pick up the pace. Suddenly, the horse stopped dead and bridled, its head twisting and stabbing the air. Shying to the right, the animal sensed danger. Herman felt it too. He made two fists and hunched over as the shell whistled and exploded close behind them.

"Get out of the wagon! Into the woods!" Tatus yelled and Herman saw his father jump from the wagon and drag his mother and Aunt Hannah down after him. They all scrambled for the shelter of the tree line. Herman heard the roar of the approaching missile, felt the blast shake the road, throw up a blanket of dirt and debris, and spray scorching shrapnel in all directions. His mother stumbled, cried out and collapsed. She was rocking back and forth on the ground in agony, clasping her ankle that was gashed and burnt by a fragment of hot flying metal. The horse was dead and everyone was cowering by the roadside: Aunt Hannah was crying, Uncle Avram was praying; Barak and Lutek were flat on their stomachs, craning their necks to see where the next shell might come from.

"We are alright. We are alright," Tatus said, but he was grey with shock. He cuddled Mamusia. She was sobbing in pain and the blood was spilling down her ankle, trickling into her best shoe. Herman looked around at the violent scene and the sight of his frightened parents. Panic hit him. Mamusia and Tatus. Look at them. In only weeks, they had aged 20 years. They looked incredibly old and feeble huddled there in the dirt. What if they die? What if the Germans kill them? He watched blood seep from the felled horse onto the snowy road. He was shivering and he wanted to crawl into the horseless wagon to hide under the blankets. Confused thoughts overtook him. What is happening to us? How did we get here?

Brazil, we have to get to Brazil. Herman suddenly remembered that his father had relatives in Brazil. That's right, some time ago, he had heard his parents talking about moving there. Then later, they had discussed how it was too late to leave, too late to get out of Poland. The window had closed on their chance to escape, they had said. Now, crouched next to the bombed-out road and showered with dirt, Herman thought about running away to Brazil. Once in a book, he had seen pictures of the hot, luxurious country and its beautiful dark-haired, dark-eyed people. Back then, he had not wanted to immigrate and leave his home in Bydgoszcz and all the things he loved: ice-skating and shopping and theater and playing in the streets with friends. Now, he was shivering from the cold outside and the shock he felt inside. I wish that we were in Brazil, he thought. I wish we had all gone while we had the chance.

Peter, their driver, had turned out to be capable and quick-witted. It was hard for the Jewish Rosenblats who had hired him to get a room each night, but Peter, a Christian, never had any problem finding a place to stay. When a Polish innkeeper asked the driver why he was working for Jews, Herman had heard Peter say that it was because they paid him well. But Herman thought it was more than that. The short, stocky Pole was a man of few words. Still, Herman could tell that under it all he was kind. He was one of those people, who just didn't see the point of hating Jews.

Now Herman watched the driver get up and brush himself off. "Wait here," he said, "I'm going to go find a new horse." Peter left them all hunkered down by the road and headed off up the lane towards the shelling. The hours ticked by. Now and then, Tatus stood in the middle of the lane and scanned the horizon. "I don't think Peter is coming back," he said finally.

"What shall we do then, Tatus?" Herman asked. "Mother is hurt."

"I know, but It's too late and too dangerous to set out on foot," Tatus said. "Your mother can't walk. We should just try and sleep in the wagon till morning."

22

Chilled to the bone, Herman huddled in the wagon with the others, sharing blankets and trying to hold in some heat. Dusk was falling when he spotted a man in the distance leading a horse with a rope. Peter came tramping towards them. He hitched the new horse to the wagon and they were off again.

Closer to Warsaw, they saw clutches of people in a panic crowding the road. Gangs of them looked to be headed towards the big city, while others trudged away from it. Herman squinted at a figure sprawled on the roadside and leaned over the side of the wagon for a closer look. A dead man! Repulsed and transfixed all at the same time, he couldn't drag himself away from the frightening sight. The man's eyes were open and staring, his skin was black, and his legs were twisted at awful angles. He finally pulled himself away to watch a group of dirty Polish soldiers. They were not marching into battle now, they were headed away from the fight, still carrying their rifles tied with string. Above them, the German Luftwaffe was precision flying, headed for their targets.

For the first time, it dawned on Herman that the Polish army was outmanned and out machined. He hadn't worried about Isydor and Abraham up until this moment. If the Germans capture them, he fretted now, they will kill them because they are Jews. He turned inward away from the, crowds, corpses, and debris littering the roads. I can't go on being the baby of the family, he thought, with the others always coddling me. Until the older ones come back, Tatus and Mamusia need me to act like a grown up.

Warsaw was crowded and lawless and the German army had beaten the Rosenblats to it. The streets were already filled with soldiers in green uniforms and rejoicing Volkedeutsch. Even crowds of raucous Poles were singing and dancing and giving the German invaders a warm welcome. Herman watched a young woman pull up her skirt and show her stocking tops to a German soldier who was smoking a cigarette and laughing. Tatus said that they were probably glad that Poland belonged to Germany now, or maybe they were just overjoyed that the war for was over before it had really begun.

Tatus decided that nothing could be worse than the insanity they found in the sprawl of a chaotic and treacherous Warsaw. Scavenging for food and a place to sleep was dangerous. Mother was in pain and limping in her ruined gold-buckled shoes. Buildings were ablaze, black smoke belching from their windows and escaping into the tumult of the streets. There was gunfire on every street corner and German soldiers were turning their guns on any looters they found robbing stores. They shouldered their rifles, peered through their sights, and picked off the plunderers as they emerged with their arms full of stolen goods.

"We are going home," Tatus announced after only a few days. Wolborz had to be safer than this hellhole. They joined another swell of refugees heading out of town and endured more days of creeping along until eventually they arrived on the outskirts of Wolborz.

As they approached Uncle Avram's house, Herman spotted them--unwelcome arrivals: truck loads of German soldiers and a black touring car of SS. Herman got a glimpse of their black uniforms and death's head insignia. He watched as a German convoy overtook them. Just ahead, one truck slowed and then stopped. Soldiers jumped down and ran at them. They stormed the wagon with such force that Herman shrank against his mother, wedging himself into her armpit. The soldiers grabbed Tatus and Uncle Avram and hurled the men off the wagon and onto the road, flat on their faces. Herman saw Uncle Avram's wide-brimmed hat fly off and wheel along the ground towards another soldier who stopped it with his foot and stomped it into the dirty snow.

"Give us your gold and diamonds," two of the soldiers yelled as they kicked the two men.

"Please, please, don't hurt us. I swear we don't have any gold or diamonds," Tatus pleaded. Crouched on the ground, he pushed his palms out to fend off more attacks. Uncle Avram was terrified; all he could do was curl up in the slush, crying.

Herman began to tremble as one of the soldiers pulled a knife from his belt. Strutting over to Uncle Avram, the soldier threw a look over his shoulder at his comrades who were cheering and egging him on with whistles and hand claps. Now he stooped and grabbed the end of the old man's white beard. He began hacking and sawing until half of it was gone. "You filthy old kike," he said. "Now you are only half a Jew aren't you?" He threw down the beard and spat on it."

Herman looked down from the wagon at the soldier staring up at them; his eyes were narrow slits of hatred. "You are all going to die," he hissed, and then he clambered back onto the truck. His comrades helped him up and they were grinning and slapping his back. One of them banged the side of the vehicle with the signal to pull out.

Mamusia and Aunt Hannah were leaning against each other, and sobbing. His cousins sat shocked and silent. Maybe they felt ashamed because they hadn't done anything to protect Uncle Avram and Tatus. Peter had stayed in his seat, just staring straight ahead during the attack. Now, he jumped down and helped the two injured men back into the wagon.

In silence, they limped the short distance to Uncle Avram's house. When they arrived, Herman's terror turned to joy. His brothers were back! All of them! He leapt from the back of the wagon and threw himself into Isydor's arms.

The Polish army, routed in only weeks, had disintegrated.

"The Germans caught us but they didn't know we were Jews, so they let us go almost at once," Abraham said. And there was Sam. Herman saw him leaning against the doorway, grinning. His hair was hanging in his eyes that always seemed to be dancing around so see where he could go next. He said that he had taken off to retrieve the family's belongings from the Bydgoszcz apartment.

"I wanted to get your silver for you, Mamusia," he told his mother who hopped on her good foot and patted his back, crying and laughing at the same time. "What happened?" she said. Sam explained that he had found their apartment commandeered by their old friend and music teacher who had enjoyed so many family dinners with the Rosenblats and who always said that Mamusia made the best potatoes. "He called me a dirty kike," Sam said, "then he warned me not to come back and ran me off with a gun."

Chapter Three
Occupation

Uncle Avram owned the tall narrow building that head-quartered the Polish police in Wolborz. One day at the end of October, two SS officers pulled up in a black car. Striding into the building, they took over a section of the offices. Who could stop them? Herman thought when he heard about it. What little he had seen of the SS was terrifying: the arrogant air, aggressive manner, the black uniforms with SS and death's head insignia—the skull and crossbones. Their carefully engineered reputation for brutality preceded them and they strode along in its wake; shoulders squared, head up, and chin out, ready to show the Jews of Wolborz what was what.

Soon after the SS rode into town, on a late afternoon in the middle of the week, Herman sat on a stool, staring out from the only window of the single room that Isydor had rented for the family. The landlord, his wife and daughter lived in the other half of the two-room house they now shared. All six Rosenblats were crammed into the tight, airless space. One room furnished with only four beds, one table, six chairs, and a broken-down dresser.

That was it. The walls were painted a depressing mustard color. But Herman didn't mind it. He did not crave privacy like his brothers. He enjoyed the closeness.

Perched on the stool, he jiggled his leg and tapped his feet on the floor, as he waited for his father and brothers to come home. The Rabbi of Wolborz was a very well known and revered religious scholar. That day, the SS had called him for a meeting, and afterwards, he had summoned the town elders to his home so he could tell them about it.

After a while, Herman stood up and sidled over to his mother, hoping she might take the hint and hug him. But she was busy. She always had a pile of chores to do. Every day, the same routine: drawing and hauling water from the communal pump in the square, packing sawdust into bricks to feed the stove, cooking and cleaning the run-down room. She had just finished peeling vegetables for their evening meal. Now, she looked up from stirring her stew and smiled at him. "They will be back soon enough, Herman," she said.

Herman climbed back on his perch to resume his lookout. He watched his mother carry her pot of vegetables to the small stove. She still limped a little from her shrapnel wound; kind of a hitch and shuffle as she walked, but she didn't seem as depressed. He turned back to the window, and spotted his father and three brothers, a dark huddle moving down the street, their jackets blowing out behind them, each one using a hand to anchor his hat in the strong wind. Herman ran to open the door, and his mother cleared the table, so that the men could sit down and give a report.

"The SS told the Rabbi that their intention is to live in harmony with the Jews," Tatus said. "As long as we follow the rules. Anyone who doesn't follow the rules will be shot." Herman saw that Tatus was trying to smile, but there was no sugar coating the message.

He remembered the word Abraham had taught him: ultimatum. Do what I say or else.

"Rule number one," Tatus went on, "all Jews must wear on their arm a blue Star of David, eight centimeters high, and stitched on a white ribbon. Avram has volunteered to make these armbands for everyone."

Abraham was pacing, too agitated to sit. He had kind eyes but they could turn intense like now when he was heated up about something. He was thin as though all his nervous energy was using him up. And his ears stuck out. He rubbed the back of the right one whenever he was thinking hard or worrying. The SS were only faking polite, he said, rubbing his ear. Everyone knew how much they despised Jews. Without a doubt, they were there to tighten the noose and make life harder. Jews were no longer allowed to listen to radios or to read newspapers, but news still made its way into the village. They had heard plenty of stories about how Nazis were now deporting Polish Jews to concentration camps, like Treblinka in the east, not just for holding but for finishing--extermination.

"Suppertime." Rose interrupted the bad news by setting down the pot of soup and a loaf of bread. After all the anxious talk, the arguing and debate about the SS and their dictates, the family settled down to eat. Tatus was hopeful. "As long as we do exactly what they tell us, "life under the SS will go on as before," he said. But Herman caught Isydor and Abraham exchanging looks across the table. They didn't look convinced.

Life did not go on as before. The rules piled up: Jews were confined to the ghetto, crowded into just three or four streets in Wolborz, away from their non-Jewish neighbors. Jews could no longer go into government buildings and hospitals. If they got sick, they would just have to die.

One day, the Rabbi asked Isydor to come and see him. "Isydor," he said, "the SS have told me that we have to create a Judenrat--a Jewish government. I want you to take the position as head of the Judenrat. The job means that you will have to appoint and oversee a staff to run the Wolburz ghetto and then report to the SS on all our affairs."

When Isydor told the family the news, Herman grinned and did a lap around the table. "That's a big honor, Isydor," he said.

"It's not an honor, Herman, it's dangerous." Isydor frowned. "It means I have to deal closely with the SS and they are unpredictable."

Jews had to wear their armbands with the Star of David, but Jewish men could still request permission to work outside the ghetto, and gentiles were allowed in to trade with them. Sometimes, Herman went with Tatus and Uncle Avram when they left to trade clothes and garment repairs for food--chicken, eggs, butter, milk and vegetables. They turned these over to the magician in the kitchen—Mamusia. She transformed the simple wages into tasty meals that were the high point of the day.

Uncle Avram was a journeyman tailor of sorts. He made the circuit of the local farms, where everyone knew him. He pedaled his trade, working away for days at a time. Whenever he could finagle it, Herman accompanied him, grabbing the chance to head out of the ghetto and revel in life outdoors. He ran through the fields, playing with the farmers' kids. He helped to feed the livestock, lifting and tossing hay in golden bails with a pitchfork from a sunny loft onto the barn floor. When he was too tired from play, he wandered indoors to sit and watch his uncle work. Always with the pins in his mouth, he found the tailor doing repairs, or fitting a jacket on a farmer who was forced to stand still and awkward with his arms stuck out like a scarecrow.

Back in the village, Herman was restless and pent up, frustrated at being tied to his mother's apron strings. She fussed and nagged him not to stray outside the ghetto where he might get a beating from the Polish police who enforced the growing list of rules and regulations. When Abraham wasn't off doing odd jobs, he worried about his little brother's empty head, and tried to tutor him a little. He made Herman practice reading and writing for at least two hours a day, but Herman tried to wriggle out of the study; he found it impossible to concentrate in the small cluttered room. He wanted out to play on the streets with the landlord's daughter and the other Jewish kids.

One day, the SS called for Isydor. They told him that as head of the Judenrat it was his job to compile and hand over to them a complete list of names and particulars of all Jews in the ghetto. Comply or suffer the consequences. Now Jews could no longer receive mail or travel outside the ghetto. For a while, farmers were still allowed to come in to trade or buy what few wares--cabinets, metalwork or tailoring that the Jews could manage to make with dwindling supplies, but eventually came complete isolation. No gentiles allowed in. No Jews allowed out. Now food was scarce, the soups thinner and less of it.

On a cold day in September, Herman stood on the banks of the nearby stream with a growing crowd of villagers. They had hurried to the water's edge after a neighbor had run through the ghetto shouting that he had seen the Rabbi's body floating there in the water. Herman tagged along. He was nervous about what he might find, but he still felt compelled to join the procession.

Until the Polish police had called it off limits, Herman had loved to play by the stream, taking long walks with his parents in the summer, watching villagers gather there on Sundays to do the wash or visit. The mothers nursed their babies and couples promenaded. Even better was the ice-skating in winter. But after the stream was forbidden, all Herman could do was stand a ways off and watch the Christian boys skate on the glassy surface. Bundled up, with red faces under their wool caps, they raced each other with one arm behind their back, until it was too cold and dark and time to go home. Skating with his brothers had been one of Herman's favorite hobbies, now it was just another thing that the Nazis insisted he wasn't allowed to do.

Today, the scene by the stream was desperate. Women were crying and wailing when they saw what had happened to the Rabbi. Herman watched a couple of young men wade into the icy water to pull out the poor old man's body. But then he looked away, afraid to see the drenched corpse lying on the bank. After a minute, he worked up the courage to peek between the legs of the men who were standing over the beaten rabbi. He saw the angry red and purple bruises that covered the old man's face. His skin was pale and grey, his lips blue, and his expression anguished, like his SS tormentors had tortured him. Herman saw the bullet holes in his clothes, too many to count. A man kneeling next to the body looked up with tears starting to fill his eyes. "The SS used him for target practice," he said, "and then they dumped him in the water."

Only a few days before on the eve of Yom Kippur, after Kold Nidre, the first prayer of the Day of Atonement, Polish police had barged into the synagogue, shouting and disrupting the service. They marched to the front, took the Rabbi by both arms and led him out, past his congregation, and away to the police station. Isydor leaned back as a Policeman jabbed a finger in his face. "You come too," he said.

At the station, Isydor tried to be diplomatic. "When will you release the Rabbi?" he asked the SS officer in charge. "When you agree to establish a Jewish police force to help keep order and a sanitation force to clean up the ghetto and keep it free of disease," the SS man said. Isydor agreed and the SS let the Rabbi go.

It was very late, but that night, Herman had lain awake, waiting for his father and Isydor. When they did come back, they brought more dismal news. "The SS released the Rabbi, but the synagogue is not to be used for prayers anymore," Tatus said. "They are going to turn it into a horse stable." Mamusia scrubbed her eyes and covered her face. Herman was 12 now and old enough to understand why she was upset. To take away his place of worship was to disrupt the sacred bond between a Jew and his God.

"Police are guarding the synagogue," Tatus said. "Nothing is to be touched. They say that they will shoot anyone who tries to take the silver or the Torahs, but the Rabbi insists that somehow the Torahs be removed and taken to safety."

The next day the street was buzzing with more news. Some brave soul had managed to get by the guards and into the synagogue to remove the Torahs and the silver ornaments that protected them. I'm happy that someone has the courage to fight back, Herman thought, but then he noticed that Isydor was tight-lipped and frowning, shaking his head like he knew that the situation would not end well.

That evening, barred from the synagogue, the Rabbi had squeezed his congregation into his home to celebrate Yom Kippur. But the night was to be a repeat performance of the previous one. The Polish police interrupted the service. Crashing through the door, angrier and more forceful this time, they grabbed the Rabbi. He smiled and nodded, trying to reassure his frightened congregation, as the police dragged him out. This time he was locked up and not released.

Later, Herman fretted as he lay next to Sam in the bed they shared. The Rabbi had been so kind to him. He hadn't gone to

Yeshiva like other boys his age, which meant he had barely learned any Hebrew. "The Rabbi was very good to me," Herman whispered to Sam. "He took me under his wing and tried to teach me how to read the Torah and ritual prayers." Sam turned and put his back to Herman in the tight space of the shared bed. Please God, Herman prayed silently, watch over the Rabbi and don't let the SS hurt him.

The following morning, his mother was a wreck. "Herman, stay on the street right in front of the house," she pleaded. "Please do not run off where I can't see you."

"Yes Mamusia," Herman agreed, but once outside, he had crept off to play down at the bakery. The bakery was a special place for Herman. On the Sabbath, it was forbidden to work or make fire or cook. And so, each Friday Herman went with his mother and the other women to carry the cholent or Sabbath stew in a pot to the baker. The baker kept the food warm for them in his ovens until the women picked it up the next day for the Sabbath meal.

On a cold day like today, Herman liked to sneak into the back of the bakery, climb up and sit on the warm ovens, until the baker chased him away. Today, he hoisted himself up on to the warm flat surface and sat with his legs dangling over the edge of the oven. He needed a quiet moment to listen to himself think. As he looked around, he saw something gleaming next to the wall. He leaned back and behind the big black oven he noticed a long glistening object pushed into a small sunken recess. He scooted back further to get a closer look. Hidden there in the narrow channel were the Torahs from the synagogue. Herman had never been so close to the sacred objects. He reached out to touch them but didn't dare. Should I take them or leave them here? he thought. What if someone sees me taking them out? Better leave them. He jumped down from the oven and ran home, pacing up and down outside the house, waiting for his father to come back.

When Tatus finally arrived home, Herman took his hand and pulled him inside. After he closed the door, he whispered in his ear. "I found the Torah scrolls behind the ovens in the bakery," he said.

"Are you sure?" His father frowned and looked puzzled.

"I'm sure." Herman noticed his mother watching them.

"Did anyone else see?" his father asked. Herman shook his head and rocked from foot to foot, waiting. He knew the news was important. Tatus pressed a finger to his lips. It was their secret. Then he put on his jacket, and took himself off to the police station. He asked to see the Rabbi and chatted about incidentals for a few minutes before leaning into the old man and whispering: "I know where the Torahs are. If we return them, the SS might let you go?" The Rabbi shook his head. "I am an old man," he said, "I will not live through the war. Keep the Torahs safe for God and for the Jews who survive. Preserve them for the next generation." After Tatus had left the prison that night, no one else had been allowed to see the Rabbi.

Now, standing next to the stream, Herman watched the men from the village lift up the Rabbi's devastated body and carry it home to be washed and prepared for burial. A group of elders went to the Polish police for permission to bury him in the Jewish cemetery on the edge of town. The next day, escorted by police, every Jew in the village joined the long snaking line on its sad trek to the cemetery. Herman walked between his mother and Abraham. It was his first funeral.

"What will we do now?" Isydor asked his father after the services.

"We can't bring a new rabbi from another town," Tatus said,

"so we will have to appoint an acting rabbi, the most learned and religious man we have among us."

But then the SS banned services altogether, forbidding any religious expression whatsoever. Now, if the Jews wanted to attend services, they had to do it in secret at their neighbors' homes. "It's too dangerous," Tatus announced to the family after a while. He didn't want them to risk it anymore, and with that, the SS had successfully put an end to the family's worship.

Death by a thousand cuts. Life in the ghetto was cramped, demoralizing and pent up. The Polish police decided to put all able-bodied men and boys in Wolborz to work widening the banks of the stream. Of course the bank did not need widening. Abraham said that the scheme was just make-work. The hard labor with picks and shovels was meant to keep the Wolborz Jews too busy, tired, and distracted to make trouble for the SS. But Herman enjoyed it. He worked with the other boys at the stream, bringing water for the men, and running small errands.

One day in the following March, the head of the Jewish police, Mr. Jabwornovksi, stopped by their room to tip off Isydor. Herman opened the door and smiled to see one of his favorite visitors, but Mr. Jabwornovski was not his usual good-natured self. He pushed past Herman to get inside. "Isydor, the SS are coming to kill you," he blurted out, the upset written all over his red, anxious face. "You should make a run for it and hide."

"Why are they coming for me?" Isydor asked.

"I don't know," Mr. Jabwornovski said. "I don't know the reason, I just know they are coming for you." Tatus stood up in a panic. He knocked over his chair. Mamusia sank into her chair, fighting back tears. Only Isydor got to work gathering up a blanket, a warm coat and a loaf of bread. He kissed everyone and was gone within minutes.

Herman waited with the family and in less than an hour, two SS arrived. They barged in without knocking. "Where is Isydor Rosenblat?" the smaller of the two barked. Always with the shouting. Herman stood glued to the spot in fear, trying to avoid looking directly at the two tormentors.

"He did not come back from his work." Tatus spoke calmly as Rose stood by the stove. She was gripping Herman's shoulders, digging her fingers into him. The SS looked around the grimy room and Herman could see their disgust.

"When he does comes back, tell him to come to the Police station," the smaller one ordered as they strode out. Soon after, a Polish policeman knocked on the door. "We are looking for Isydor," the man said like he could care less. Tatus repeated the alibi. "He hasn't come by home yet."

The next morning, when Herman got up, his mother looked pale. "Herman, there will be a funeral today," Mamusia said. "Mr. Jabwornovski is dead. When the SS couldn't find Isydor, they came for Mr. Jabwornovski instead. They took him out to the marketplace and…" Mamusia broke down before she could finish. "and they shot him." It took her a few sobbing starts before she could finally get the words out.

In the procession to the cemetery, Herman turned to his father with the same old question: "Why do the Germans want to destroy all the Jews?"

"Hitler hates everybody, especially Jews," Tatus said, tenting his fingers, looking for a way to make the explanation palatable. "He wants to make Germany the greatest power in the world and to brag to Germans that he does great deeds for them like ridding the Fatherland of Jews and other bad elements, so they can feel strong in their nationalistic pride."

Herman didn't understand any of it. How does it make the

Germans great to murder Jews? he thought. The SS had killed two of his favorite people. First, the Rabbi--a revered man, always gentle, and kind enough to help him learn his religion and how to be a good Jew. And now, Mr. Jabwornovksi, who was also a very good man. Isn't everyone here in mourning at his funeral? There is his wife. She is heart broken and no one can make her feel better. A group of weeping neighbors, all in black, was huddled around her, patting and stroking, and clutching her in spasms of anguished embrace. And Isydor. He had tried to go along with everything that the SS had told him to do, but now he was forced into hiding and they didn't even know why.

Isydor stayed away until a new SS detail arrived. No one bothered to tell them that he was on the wanted list and the Polish police seemed just as happy to keep the information to themselves. Two weeks after he first took off into hiding, Isydor came quietly into their room. When Herman looked up and saw him, Isydor put his finger to his lips. Shush. Then he crept up behind Mamusia who had her back turned, washing pots. She threw up her arms and shrieked: "Thank God, Isydor. Thank God, you've come home." Herman laughed as he watched her hold onto his brother, patting his back, kissing him, and buzzing around him for the rest of the afternoon. The next day, Isydor was back to running the Wolborz Judenrat.

Chapter Four
Oprah

Oprah's producer called again. The same request: Oprah was inviting Herman to come on the show to discuss the situation and explain himself. Herman still hedged. He really didn't think he could do it. He'd given it some thought. But everyone had advised him not to. His lawyer had warned against it, definitely not. "Zip it, Herman, and keep it zipped," Harry told him. "Enough harm has been done already."

The following Friday, at four o'clock, Herman switched on the TV. "I don't want to see," Roma called through the hatch in the kitchen wall. Her head was tilted to one side so Herman could hear her through the opening and see the no-no-no look on her face. She was taking the situation hard. Dirty looks from the neighbors every time they ventured out to Publix for groceries or for a walk down by the water or out to the mall. And the hate mail was still coming.

When Herman took the letter from the mailbox yesterday and saw the crude swastikas drawn on the envelope, he knew what to expect. Was the post office allowed to deliver something like this? Or did it just slide through the sorting machine unnoticed by the postal workers? They couldn't look at everything, Herman supposed. He opened it: "You dirty, lying Jew bastard. They should have shoved you in the ovens with the rest of them..." No point reading the rest. Herman refolded the letter with its crude scrawl of obscenities and put it back in the envelope.

He didn't throw the letter away, but his thought wasn't to save it as evidence. Of what? Evidence that there are still plenty of people who hate Jews? So what's new? He set it on top of a pile of papers on his desk. How can it hurt me? Hate? I had the mother lode. Got my anti-Semitism straight from the experts--the SS. They wrote the manual. Everyone else is just a tinny imitation. He didn't show the letter to Roma. But, it was there on the desk in plain view, flashing its swastikas. She won't open it, he thought. He had seen her glance at it that morning. "What's that?" she asked.

"Nothing," Herman said. After 50 years of marriage, they both knew the code: don't ask, don't tell. But something else had spooked Roma today: the young reporter who got through the small security station in front of their apartment building. She had knocked on the door right before lunch and stood there holding a note pad. Roma had opened the inside door and squinted to look through the screen.

"I'm looking for Roma and Herman Rosenblat," the young woman said.

"They don't live here." Roma closed the door and dashed into the bedroom. The reporter was not brazen enough to knock again after Roma shut the door on her chutzpah. I won't follow her into the bedroom, Herman decided. Just leave her alone. He stood outside the bedroom, his ear pressed to the closed door, listening for any crying. No sound. He left and then tiptoed back at intervals to listen again. He had dozed off by the time she came out an hour later. She was making noise in the kitchen. "Coffee and Danish?" she called to him.

"Yes please dear." She's all right, he thought. That is why he had risked switching on Oprah. He thought Roma could handle it in the background. But she was more rattled than he realized. "I don't want to hear." Again her head on an angle, framed by the hatch. Her voice firm. "Please, dear, can you go in the bedroom?" he said, trying to smooth it. She turned the faucet. The running water was loud.

Today's show was "Friday, Live in Chicago". There was Oprah sitting with her guest panel at a table, people Herman didn't recognize. Oh wait. That one on the end was Oprah's friend. Gail? The panel was talking about different stories and news. "And later, we will be bringing you an update on the Herman Rosenblat story," Oprah said into the camera. She was looking right at Herman. The water in the kitchen ran even louder.

A plane had crashed landed on the Hudson River in New York a few days back. No one was hurt. The pilot was some mensch who got everybody out alive. Oprah's panel discussed it for a while. Then more kibitzing. Things that didn't mean anything to Herman. It was almost three quarters through the show when Oprah resumed the subject of Herman Rosenblat. She replayed clips of Herman and Roma's appearance. "We asked Herman repeatedly to come on the show today to talk to us, but he declined," Oprah said in a steady TV voice.

That last time we were there on the show, Herman remembered, Oprah was so kind to us. He still had a special glossy photograph of the great lady taken with Roma and himself, framed and hanging in his office, a real prized possession. All the producers and staff were so thoughtful. He and Roma had been guests for a special Valentine's Day show. Billed by Oprah, or the producer, or whoever made up the script, as a follow-up to the greatest love story ever told. That's what Oprah had called Herman and Roma's love story when she first revealed it on her show. That had to be what? Thirteen years ago? It was the first time that they had gone on the program.

For the second appearance, the one on Valentine's Day, the show staff had arranged for Herman and Roma to fly to Chicago and to stay in such a nice hotel. Like an apartment--a sitting room, big bedroom, and a huge tiled bathroom, as big as Herman's office. Like a honeymoon suite. It was 2008. Herman and Roma had been married for 50 years, a golden anniversary. The next day, a car brought them to the studio. A producer took Herman to one side. "Oprah is going to remind the audience of how you met-- your love story. And then she is going to cue your surprise, okay?" Herman nodded and patted his pocket. He had the box tucked safely in there.

So much life and activity around him, Herman felt renewed by the energy on the set of the show. Roma hadn't been feeling well. A touch of depression but the excitement was really lifting her spirits. Herman looked at her. She had been to the beauty shop. Hair so nice. Her best clothes. A little lipstick. Herman loved a crowd, enjoyed an audience. Seize the moment, he always thought, and shake the life out of it. Why not? Hadn't he seen lives snuffed out? Thousands, old and young, murdered before they had the chance to live. Don't waste the day. Live it for those who can't.

There was a break in taping and Herman and Roma were led onto the set and seated in chairs next to Oprah. She was a pretty woman with lots of makeup and false eyelashes for the television cameras. She was businesslike but she seemed kind. Knew how to be a person with people. A producer with a clipboard and a headset signaled that it was time to start taping again.

Oprah looked into the camera and retold the love story of Herman and Roma Rosenblat that she had first shared over a decade ago. Herman could see that there were mostly ladies in the audience. All dressed up too--like a party. Sure, coming on Oprah was a special occasion like a wedding or a celebration. A once-in-a-lifetime event. He had been a guest twice. Herman watched the women as they listened to Oprah—their hero. Many were blinking away tears. Others dabbed with a hankie, trying not to smear the makeup. His story moved them. It proved that even in the worst conditions there was always hope. That love conquers all. It defeats even the worst evil in the world.

"And you want so say what, Herman?" Oprah looked at him. He was not nervous. He stood up and in front of Roma, took the small blue velvet box out of his pocket, and knelt down on one knee. Oy! Not so easy at 78. He snapped opened the box and presented the ring. He had picked it out himself at JC Penney in the mall; not the close one, the better one, out by the airport. Roma was surprised, patting her neck and laughing; her eyes shining. So thrilled.

"Roma, as this ring has no end, so my love for you has no end," Herman said and he meant it. Meant it with all his heart.

Chapter Five
Typhus

By May 1942, Herman had been living with his family in the cramped, dirty and depressing conditions of their one room in the Wolborz ghetto for more than two and a half years. One morning, he was watching Tatus, as he tried to get out of bed. He looked really sick, squeezing his eyes shut and moaning. He had a fever, and a really terrible headache, he said, and his muscles hurt so bad. He felt awful, just awful.

"Stay, stay, stay," Mamusia said and pushed Tatus down whenever he tried to get up. Tatus finally gave in and fell back on the bed. He stayed there all day, resting and trying not to flail around in the heat and the squalor of the room. His mattress was practically alive, infested with an army of lice that they couldn't shift. In pain, but uncomplaining, he just let the odd moan escape from his dry slack mouth.

Before supper, Isydor palmed his father's brow. "Hot and clammy," he said. The oldest son looked up and down the length of his sick father, trying to settle on what he could do to help a man so poorly, in surroundings so miserable, and with aid so nonexistent.

Tatus is only 59 but he looks ancient. He's so thin, and undernour-ished, Herman thought. He's exhausted from working so hard. Even before the war he slaved, trying to provide for us, and now it hurts him. It hurt him to see the things that are happening to the Jews and to our family.

Herman stood off to the side and watched his brother. Isydor was always really thoughtful and careful. His hair is starting to thin now, Herman thought. Maybe one day it will go completely bald on the crown, just like Tatus. Isydor is like Tatus in many ways, come to think of it. Calm and reliable. He always knows what to do next. And, he's neat and organized, no matter what the task, from packing a suitcase to running the ghetto.

"Let's wait a while to see if the fever breaks," Isydor said after he had stood watching his father for while. Now, Tatus was grabbed by one of the violent coughing attacks that had come on with his other symptoms. His body jerked and spasmed and his fists curled and squeezed. It hurt Herman to watch him.

Work was still underway to widen the stream. Running up and down, fetching water and running errands, usually helped Herman forget his problems and burn off his nervous energy. He liked being outdoors with the grown ups. Even though it was hard work, the men kept each other's spirits up with their joking and kibitzing, whenever the police were out of earshot. But for the next few days, Herman was joyless. He worked without his usual enthusiasm, loading loose soil into a large bucket. His arms pulled straight by the weight, he hauled the container with both hands to a large growing pile of earth, where he dumped it. As he worked he fretted about Tatus. Now and then, he stopped and set down the heavy bucket, halted in his tracks by a heavier worry pressing down on his young shoulders.

Herman pictured his father in the bed at home, his usual

energy and good humor drained out of him. Tatus is sick but he won't die, he kept telling himself. He is sick, but he will get better. Herman was still too young to know that life can override and cancel any hope, wish, or prayer, no matter how fervently made. If you love someone as much as I love Tatus, he told himself, then that means they won't die and leave you.

In the late afternoons, Herman sprinted home, hoping to find the patient sitting up at least. But Tatus was getting sicker, shrinking in the bed, taking up less room on the lousy mattress. Saying less and sleeping more; an awful, comfortless sleep. There was no break in his symptoms. Wolborz had no Jewish doctor; officially, Jews were not allowed to practice medicine anymore, so they called uncle Avram, who had lived in the village forever and was on good terms with the gentile doctor. "I will ask him to come late tonight," Uncle Avram said, but Tatus barely heard him and just gazed off with red-rimmed eyes.

The doctor crept in for a visit in the middle of the night. The SS would shoot him if they caught him tending to a Jew. If Jews got sick, they were supposed to die. Mamusia had strung up a curtain on a wire to divide the single room. It sagged in the middle and didn't really work as an effective quarantine. After a few minutes, the doctor was finished with his examination and came out from behind the curtain. "Typhus," he announced. The ghetto was dirty and crowded and typhus was rampant now. "Place compresses on his head." The doctor sounded all business. "Keep him and his bedding as clean as you can. All of you, wash your hands before and after touching him. I'll try and come back tomorrow night with some medication." Then, he left, looking uneasy.

When the doctor had gone, Herman sat with Isydor. "Will Tatus get better?" he asked. Isydor ignored him, so Herman looked out of the window, hoping no one would see how shaken he was. The next night, the doctor came back with medication. He barely stopped long enough to explain the directions, before his fear of being caught in the home of a Jew propelled him back out into the night.

The family tended to the patient as best they could. Herman watched Mamusia trying to get a thin soup or water down him, slowly tipping liquid from the spoon through his dry, cracked lips and into his mouth. She soaked strips of an old sheet in a basin of cold water and gently pressed the cool compresses against his bony face and thin, scaly limbs. Every day, she chased Herman out of the room and down to the stream, but when he was home, he watched her care for Tatus and tried to stay out of her way. Sometimes, Herman sat near his father's bed with his book open on his lap just watching him sleep. It frightened him to see how awful he looked. Like a dead man. I don't care, Herman thought, as long as he is still here where I can see him.

Tatus was not responding to the doctor's medications and his body was covered with a pinkish rash. "Isydor, how did father get typhus?" Herman asked one day. He knew his oldest brother was like a doctor, because he was a dentist, and he had studied basic medicine.

"He got it from the lice," Isydor said. The entire family was infested, eaten alive and constantly scratching the bites. "Bacteria from the lice gets scratched into the wound and causes the infection," Isydor explained. It was hard to stay clean. There was no running water in the house and they had to share a dirty outhouse with their neighbors. Herman took his turn with Mamusia and the others, trekking to the communal pump in the Wolborz marketplace, to haul water. They heated it on the stove so they could wash themselves. They were all lousy but only Tatus had succumbed to typhus. He was growing weaker and thinner, the awful angles of his knees and elbows sticking through his rumpled, sour smelling bed shirt.

One day, Herman snuck behind the curtain and sat next to Tatus, reading aloud from the book that Abraham made him study. His eyes kept skidding off the lines of neat black letters and he couldn't concentrate, too many distractions. Too much worry. He was falling behind in his education and even though this was his 13th year, no bar mitzvah was possible. His rite of passage into manhood would have to be foregone; just a small personal loss among the massive losses that were mounting for his people. Herman sat with his father but said nothing for a while because Tatus seemed unusually comfortable and quiet. Herman's eyes kept escaping the page of his book to rest on his father, a restless checking back and forth. "Tatus, how are you?" he asked finally.

"Son, I think God wants me to be with him," Tatus said and his directness stung Herman.

"But I don't want you to die." Herman dropped his book to scurry over and perch on the bed, unstitched by the quiet way his father had surrendered to the idea of his own death. Somewhere, deep down, Herman still believed that his parents had the power to make things come right the way they always used to before the war started.

"If God wants you, son, there is nothing to do but obey," Tatus said, and he did not sound even a little bit upset or afraid. "Herman, if you get through this war, I want you to be happy. Don't be bitter. Don't bear a grudge. And always tolerate others. It's no use to be angry and make yourself unhappy. Do you understand?" Herman nodded, although he didn't really understand. He bent down to kiss his father and pushed his face into his nightshirt with its awful stale smell. Tatus didn't sound like his old self with all this talk of giving up and now he looked too tired to smile even. He just rested a soft gaze from his gentle brown eyes on Herman.

The next day, Tatus died in Mamusia's arms. Herman came back from work at the stream to find his father's body laid out on the bed, washed, and dressed in threadbare clothes and his prayer shawl. He looked emaciated and haggard, his eyelids closed over sunken eyes. Herman stared down at the still figure and did not recognize him.

Tatus' body was taken to a grave at the Jewish cemetery. The men lowered his corpse, unprotected by a coffin, into the hole. The service commenced and mourners said Kaddish--prayers for the dead. As Herman listened to the incantations in the unfamiliar Hebrew, the finality of what had happened started to sink in. The lively music of their family quartet was far away now, faded to silence. The intimate chatter of Shabbat dinners ended. The smiles of a loving father were finished. Herman heard the dirt falling into the hole. Men were shoveling damp earth on top of Tatus. He stepped forward and saw the black soil land and spray over his Father's white tallis like specks of darkness gathering to smother any prayers he might have given up to his God.

Herman felt his first real grief, intense and terrifying, break over him as he watched the cruel disposal of his beloved father. I'll never see Tatus again, he thought, as panic crowded his mind and muscled away all other thoughts. He wanted to run to his father to cry out the heartbreak of his loss. He could not dislodge it from his mind—the awful realization: Tatus is dead at the bottom of that hole and he is never coming back to me.

The pain took Herman over and built to a crescendo of hysteria. He held his breath and did not know how to stop it—the panic. He was distraught and unable to restrain himself like the other mourners. Like his mother. She had collapsed against Isydor and her face was screwed up with pain, but she was not convulsed like Herman by this new, awful, mad energy of grief. Herman jumped into his father's grave. But now he was there, what could he do? He wanted to be saved. He felt his brothers' arms reach in, grab hold of his flailing, spastic limbs, and hoist him from the hole. He was wailing, but he gave in to his rescue. On the walk home, he turned silent and numb with shock.

Back at the house, the acting Rabbi cornered Herman. "God took your father because he loved him," he said.

"Then God must hate you and me to leave us here," Herman replied. This grim insight was almost the only thing that he muttered during the next week as he sat Shiva—the long period of mourning with family for his father. In the drag of hours, he had plenty of time to contemplate the terrifying disintegration of his life that was taking place. He knew that he would never be relaxed and carefree again. Fear and anxiety would be everywhere now.

Chapter Six
Selection

The man showing them to their new living quarters was dirty and surly. Herman tried to peer around him, as he opened the door to a single room, 15 by 20 feet wide. Piss, rancid and bitter, and other foul smells, hit Herman's nostrils and intensified his disgust at the sight of the dismal set up inside: just two beds with chipped and dented metal frames. Filthy striped mattresses with the ticking bursting out in the spots where they were worn through. They were covered with a pattern of stain upon stain of different sizes and shapes: blood, urine, and who knew what else. A table, a few chairs and a cupboard, nothing more, except for the vermin. Herman could not see the lice and the maggots but he knew that they were there. The cockroaches were in plain sight, set scurrying by the intruders.

Mamusia gave it all little more than a glance. Herman could see that she was not thinking about how to make the best of it; how to clean the place and create even a hint of home that she had always devoted herself to making for her family. She listed towards a greasy, rickety chair and slumped down. She could not cope. Losing Tatus had been too much. In the last three months, Herman had watched her retreat into her grief and despair. Sometimes he stroked her arm or grabbed her hand and rubbed it to try and kindle her will to go on and be happy again. And then she would she look at him, trying to work her face into a smile.

"It's okay, Herman. As long as I have you," she said, "as long as I have my children, I will be alright." But now, she looked like a babcia, an old woman. The ones who are finished with life and spend their days waiting; children gone; energy spent, purpose forgotten.

All eyes were on Isydor. As usual, he was making a plan. "Uncle Avram, Aunt Hannah, you take one bed," he said, pointing to one of the two wrecks. "Herman, mother and Samek, you take the other. Abraham, Lutek, Barak and I will sleep on the floor. We can go looking for blankets and pillows tomorrow and food. And work." He punched the last word. "We stand more chance if we make ourselves useful." Isydor didn't have to spell it out. Everyone understood what he meant. The last 24 hours had pointed toward a brutal new direction for their lives.

Four days earlier, the SS had called Isydor to the Police Station with new orders: Assemble all the Jews in Wolborz with their belongings in the marketplace two days from now at 8 AM. Anyone late or attempting to hang behind will be shot. Isydor made the rounds, giving the orders, trying to calm his neighbors' fears and answer questions, although he really knew no more than anyone else. "It will be alright, just be in the marketplace on time. Pack what you can. Don't be late. Don't worry," Isydor told everyone, knowing full well that the last command was futile. There was every reason to be afraid.

Two days later at 8 AM, almost 400 Jews gathered in the Wolborz marketplace. It was mid August and already growing hot.

Old people sat on their suitcases. Anxious women dangled their babies. Kids played, running back and forth, looking for diversions, and pulling away from short-tempered mothers, as the interminable wait stretched on. People wandered over to the pump to get a drink or cool their faces.

Herman watched as horse-drawn wagons with Polish drivers clattered into the square. Then came the orders: everyone line up to be checked against the census list and climb quietly into the wagons. No belongings. This last command kicked off panic and the women started crying. They had been told they could bring their possessions. That's how they knew life would continue wherever it was they were going. Everyone knew where Jews separated from their belongings wound up. There was uproar. The villagers were spooked like caged creatures that smell a wild animal near the pen.

The SS were brutal; polite was long gone. They checked people against the lists and then herded them into wagons--20 per wagon. It was slow going. Despite the warnings, some villagers had hung back, stayed home or tried to hide. The Polish Police were sent to ferret them out and drag them to the marketplace. Eventually around 1 PM, chaos gave way to a terror-induced order and the wagons were off. But where? Someone said to Piotrkow, 15 miles away. There was a large Jewish ghetto in Piotrkow. The good news was passed along like a package and it seemed to calm people. They were headed towards the safety of more Jews.

The wagons were flanked by SS on motorcycles. They revved their engines. Cursed and screamed as they drove their human livestock forward. The desperate caravan moved out, but it kept running into stops. A few miles down the road, a group of new soldiers on motorcycles caught up with them. Herman saw the telltale SA on their belts--Sturmabteiling--storm troopers. Abraham had told him about them. They were in charge of concentration camps until the SS took over.

"All gold and jewelry, pass it forward," the SA screamed. "All valuables, surrender them now. We will shoot anyone who does not turn over their valuables." No one had much anymore. Everything of any value had been confiscated already. Herman watched the people in his wagon. A few women struggled to work wedding bands off their fingers. Others unhooked the odd locket or pocket watch. The small, forced collection was taken up and handed over to the SA man. He cupped his gloved hands, trapped the bits and pieces of jewelry, and then carried them off.

There was an order to move on, but soon after came another stop. Herman peered over the side of the wagon. What was the hold-up? A Pole was walking towards the SS, flanked by two men. "Juden," the man said, jabbing his thumbs out to point at the men on either side of him. SS grabbed the two men and began marching them into the woods, prodding and shoving them forward with the nose of their guns. Herman watched Isydor pushing his way to the back of the wagon. He jumped down. "I want those men included in our transport," he told the officer, calmly but firmly. Two shots rang out from over by the trees; a murder of crows took sudden violent flight and cawed loudly. "Oh, they can't come with you." The SS officer smirked at Isydor. "Would you like to go with them?"

"Get back in the wagon, Isydor," Abraham called out.

It took almost six hours to cover the 15 miles to Piotrkow. When they arrived, everyone from Wolborz was led into the synagogue. Herman looked around the temple. No holy hush today. It was a madhouse. The SS had cast their net and trawled for every Jew within the surrounding areas. Like the people of Wolborz, Jewish communities from nearby Tuszyn, Serock, Przygtow, Sulejow, Rozprza and Kamiensk had been caught, hauled and dumped in Piotrkow. The synagogue had been transformed into a holding pen and clearing house. Packed in like sardines, weary families camped out on whatever postage stamp of floor they could secure. Others had no choice but to stand. The four Rosenblat brothers and two cousins surrounded their three elders, Uncle Avram, Aunt Hannah and Mamusia, and elbowed their way to a spot in the corner of the building.

They tried to settle in. Mamusia offered Herman a crust of bread, no water. He ate it and then fell into daydreaming to escape the wail of desperate mothers and the hungry unsettled screams of infants and small children. He watched men pray. Inspired by their surroundings, they were davening and muttering. Rocking to their own internal rhythm, it looked like they were trying to rise above the tumult of human suffering that surrounded them, and unite with God. We are in God's temple, but where is God? Herman thought. He looked towards the arc of the Torahs but it was empty. Maybe that's why God is not here.

The light in the synagogue was failing and a dark umbra began to fall on the crowd imprisoned inside. Night seemed to tamp down the cries, but not the whispers. "They are going to kill us." Herman caught the frightening words as they buzzed like an electric hum across the sea of bodies. He looked up at his mother to see if she still had the power to neutralize the dread. She smiled at him. "Go to sleep, Herman." How could he? It seemed like an impossible request, but within minutes, exhausted from the travel, and the misery of the day, he turned his attention away from the scene in this new staging area of hell, and slipped into the oblivion of sleep. But the SS followed him. They were striking Tatuś, as he lay helpless like a broken puppet on the bed in Wolborz. He was dead but they still beat on him. Overkill. "Father is dead,"

Herman cried. "Tatus is dead. Leave him alone." The Germans can't hurt him, he told himself in his dream. He opened his eyes and tears were leaking from the corners.

All through the next morning, the SS and Polish police performed a roll call, summoning the communities they had corralled in the synagogue. Herman would learn that every ordeal from now on would begin and end with roll call. The SS were maniacal about Appell, driven by an obsessive need to break and harass by counting and controlling their victims. After a few hours, it was their turn to leave. The people from Wolborz were called, gathered, and then marched out of the synagogue and towards a gate in a barbed wire fence. Here they were turned over to the waiting Jewish police and members of the Piotrkow Judenrat. Their surly, unresponsive guide was assigned to bring them to their new home, the stinking fleapit where they congregated now.

Herman saw his mother stand, fired up a little by Isydor's plan. She looked around the room and noticed a broom in the corner. She pulled off her best coat; it was a rag now. Striding over to the broom, she picked it up and began sweeping, kicking up not just dust but dirt. This was not a cattle wagon. It was not the floor of a synagogue. This hole was their new home. Their world might be collapsing, the space around them contracting, but as long as she had breath, Rose would create a home for her children.

Next morning, when Herman awoke, he heard the comforting buzz of activity. Everyone was up already and Mamusia was cutting bread for breakfast. Sam, always up first, had scavenged for food and fuel for the small wood stove. Herman wanted to go out and explore. "Stay by us," his mother said.

"Oh, come on," Herman begged, "just in front of the building."

Abraham got sick of the whining. "Mother, let him go," he said. Then he eyed Herman. "Stay where we can find you."

Right out front, Herman found a small gang of kids on the street. They were thin and dirty but they had organized a game and lost themselves in it. They were chasing each other in and out of buildings. Herman hung back for a while until eventually a small kid with a flat cap invited him to join in. The kid showed him the lay of the land. "Piotrkow main ghetto is over there," he said pointing some ways off. "All Jews from the other towns are in here, the small ghetto." Ah, so they were in a ghetto within a ghetto, Herman realized. The streets were lined with rows of run-down, abused and damaged buildings. He saw holes punched like gaping mouths through many of the walls to create small makeshift tunnels so people didn't have to venture out onto the street to walk. It looked like travel was safer and easier, moving from building to building through the succession of holes. Now, Herman ran the tunnels with his new friends; they forgot the danger and misery all around them and raced back and forth, whooping and laughing, like a train of dirty ragamuffins.

The family settled into their room and a few days later, Isydor came home with shocking news. "The entire town of Radamsko has been sent to Treblinka to be gassed," he said. "The whole town murdered." Everyone clamped their hands to their mouths and Mamusia grabbed a chair for support. "We have to get jobs," Isydor said. Striding around the room, he stressed how important it was for the men to find work. "We have to make ourselves useful to the Germans either at the Bugaj lumberyard or at the Hortensja and Kara glass factories." Herman began to brood. Isydor doesn't try to protect the women and me from frightening news any more, he thought. Innocence is over. Survival is all that matters.

On a cool day in early September, Herman, his brothers and two cousins loitered with a gang of men selected for work. Shoulders hunched up, hands shoved in pockets to keep warm, they hung around at the exit of the ghetto. They were expert at waiting. Finally, the Police marched them down to the river Bug and the Bugaj lumberyard, home to the massive Dietrich & Fischer wood-working factory. Inside the factory, Herman inhaled the smell of sawdust and newly milled wood. It smelled good. He was feeling scared and curious all at once. A Polish policeman came and lined them up, then worked his way down the line demanding to know each man's age and occupation.

"I am Isydor, 31. I am a dentist."

"Good, you can treat the police and firemen. You?"

"I am Samuel. I am 20 and I can fix motor cars," Sam said.

"Good, you can work in the garage. You three?" The Polish policeman pointed at Abraham, Lutek and Barak. They were all strong, they said, and could do any job.

"What about the young one? How old are you, kid?"

"I am thirteen." Herman was too afraid to lie.

"He's too young to work. He has to go back to the ghetto," the Policeman insisted.

"If he goes back, then we all go back. He knows how to work," Isydor said like he meant business.

"Okay." The Policeman shrugged and told the others where to go.

"You come with me." He pointed to Herman. Afraid to be separated from the others, Herman eyed Isydor.

"It's alright, you can go. You'll be okay. We will meet you outside at home time." Isydor reassured him.

The policeman took Herman to the paint shop, where a hand-ful of quiet workers were painting stretchers and marking them with the initials D & F. He turned him over to apprentice with an older Jew. For a while, Herman watched in silence. It was almost hypnotic the way that the man applied red paint with his brush then stretched it out and feathered it into the wood. He had long, fine, paint-stained fingers, and he held the brush with a certain grace. "You do that very well," Herman said after a few minutes. "I used to be an artist, the man smiled at him, and then showed him how to work the spray gun.

Now, as official workers of the German war effort, Herman's brothers had work papers stamped with a swastika and a ration card that got the family enough food to get by, just. Work, food, a place to stay, Herman took stock after a couple of weeks. Maybe things were not so bad after all. But he was still too young to analyze the events of his life, to do anything other than take the days one at a time as though they were autumn leaves falling one by one from the branches of a dying tree.

If Herman had been able to trace the emerging patterns in the new painful weave of his family's life, he would have realized by now that even periods of relative calm were only a prelude to more suffering. Like the deep silence between lightening flashes in a thunderstorm, the calming first weeks of work in the Bugaj lumberyard were just a lull before the next devastating strike.

On the morning of October 14, 1942, a general curfew was called in the Piotrkow ghetto. Only members of work details and those employed at the woodworking and glass factories were allowed to leave for work. In their room, Isydor countermanded the order. Everyone was to stay home, he said. Herman looked out of the window. Soon, the Polish and Jewish police, the SS and their dogs were on parade outside. Bullhorns screamed out directions: "Bring your belongings and proceed to the Umschlagplatz." His family had no choice but to go down into the street. Once there, they were caught in the crush headed to an assembly point not far from the railroad siding where cattle cars were being loaded with people.

A man Isydor knew caught up with them on the street. "They say we are being deported to a labor camp in the east," he said, "but it's Treblinka we're really headed for. We are all going to Treblinka." The neighbor gave a grim smile like a losing player in a high-stakes poker game. The man knew there was no way to win. He looked ready to set down his bad hand.

Herman took his mother's arm. Isydor helped Uncle Avram and Aunt Hannah who were struggling to keep up with the press of bodies that flowed like a torrent, driven by shrill, incessant commands, towards the assembly points and railroad siding. They tagged onto the end of a crowd that was winding its way to a series of SS stations. Officers prowled among the crowd. "We have work papers." Isydor handed the cards to an SS who inspected them and waved the grown Rosenblat men to the right.

"You, how old?" The SS officer pointed at Herman.

"Tell him you are 16." Herman heard Isydor mutter the direction close to his ear.

"I am 16," Herman said and the officer flicked his finger. Herman was free to join his brothers. Mamusia, Uncle Avram and Aunt Hannah were next. "Over there," the SS said, pointing to the left with calm, diabolical efficiency, and just like that, they were separated. Herman was trying to fathom what the two groups meant. On the right, his side, he saw men already scurrying back in the direction of the small ghetto. Where are Mamusia and the others on the left going? he thought. In the chaos and tearing apart of families, Herman saw an SS guiding his mother, aunt and uncle in the direction of cattle cars lined up on the rails.

"Put down all belongings and get in the cars." Herman heard officers in the distance, repeating their orders with hypnotic frequency. "Put down all belongings and get in the cars." Now he felt panic squeeze his neck like a choke chain. There was wailing all around him, an awful howling chorus of screams and sobs, futile pleas to God, and the begging of SS for mercy.

Herman watched a woman. She was clutching her little girl's hand and beseeching an SS to let her go with her husband. She pointed to where he stood, hunched forward and afraid, watching and waiting. But Herman could tell that her crying and hysterical high-pitched cries were just making the SS man more enraged. He wanted her to shut up and comply. Herman saw him lift his stick and strike the woman on the side of her head, then another blow to her shoulder. She was bleeding and screaming in pain, pulling her child into the folds of her coat. Next, the SS hit the child who crumpled, screaming, against her mother. The distraught father now dashed towards them. He put his arms around his bloodied wife and child as the SS swung at them. Slashing with his stick, the officer herded the trio forward. The husband refused to leave his injured, desperate wife. He would go where she went—wherever it might be.

Now, the SS man was on a roll. His appetite whetted, he kept lashing out. Like a good farmer swinging a sickle, he cut a swathe through the crowd, hitting out at the weak, the weeping and the dazed. He held nothing back. His blows were indiscriminate but well timed, hitting his targets--the heads and shoulders of old men, women and children. See what begging and pleading gets you. Get moving towards the cattle cars.

Herman was terrified. He saw more men break ranks from safety on the right to dash towards danger on the left, rushing to reunite with wives and children. They refused to be ripped away from the family they cherished more than life. Okay, the SS shrugged, and made room for the defectors in the growing fold selected for extermination. They were welcome to go.

The men's actions and his own terror galvanized Herman.

"Mamusia!" he called out and pushed his way through the thickening layers of bodies between him and his mother and wrapped his arms round her waist. "I want to come with you."

"No, Herman, go with your brothers," she said calmly. He felt fingers squeezing his upper arm as Abraham tried to pull him away. "Herman, come with us."

"Mother." Herman yanked his arm free and attached himself to his mother again. She was eyeing an SS a few yards away, but for now, he seemed focused elsewhere.

"Herman, stop being an nuisance. Get over there with your brothers," Mamusia said and she sounded anxious. Abraham was pulling him again. Herman was angry, his adrenalin pumping, as he pulled to break free of Abraham's grip and stand with Mamusia.

"Herman." His mother's voice rose. "I am sick of you. Get over there with your brothers."

What?_ There was something in her tone that made Herman stop. She had never sounded so cold and angry with him.

"Herman, I do not love you. I want you to get away from me and go over there with your brothers. I do not want you with me. Now go." Awful words that he couldn't understand. He was shocked and unable to move. Easy for Abraham to drag him off now, but Herman never took his eyes off his mother even though she had put her back to him. With his every retreating step, he kept his eyes on her, twisting to look back over his shoulder as she moved in and out of view while the crowd between them swelled. "Mamusia," he called and he was crying now like a little boy. I want to see my mother. Why won't she turn? He had a chance for only one more glimpse before the frantic, undulating mass swallowed her up. There was her face. He could see it. She was looking after him and she was crying too.

Chapter Seven
Forced Labor

How long to process and pack 22,000 Jews into cattle cars and move them out? Herman and his brothers watched the SS accomplish the grotesque feat in about seven days. Most deportees were sent to Treblinka, the gates yawning wide with welcome; the gas chambers operating with marvelous efficiency. Herman was among only 1,700 or so strong men and boys, and a few women and girls, who were spared. They were confined to the Block, a couple of streets, hemmed in by barbed wire, all that remained of Piotrkow's small ghetto now that it had been emptied and cleansed of Jews. The human remnants left behind were forced labor for local Piotrkow factories, important to the Nazi war effort: the Dietrich & Fischer wood works at the Bugaj lumberyards and the Hortensja and Kara glass factories.

The night his mother was sent away, Herman was too numb, his mind too slow moving to fully take it all in. We are six not nine now, he realized. The family elders are gone. Herman climbed into the bed that he shared with Isydor. His brother hugged him and rubbed his arms to try and generate heat and rouse him from his shock. "Herman, don't think about bad things. Think about good things," Isydor said.

"What good things?" Herman was desperate for Isydor, who seemed to understand the meanings and outcomes of all things, to make sense of the nightmare. Good things? Could Tatus and Mamusia somehow come back? Was this ordeal just a strange hiccup in a life, which seemed perfect, more or less, until the war began? Would his life somehow right itself, like a spinning top that wobbled but then straightened up on its tip?

"Be grateful that we are still alive, still together," Isydor said.

"Is Mamusia still alive?" Herman asked.

"Go to sleep Herman." Isydor rubbed his brother's head.

Herman had always dreamed. In the quiet embrace of still night, or in the reveries of daytime, dreams had come to him often. And they often lingered with him after he awoke. Nighttime visions and nocturnal stories that he liked to replay and savor come morning.

But this night was a black night, the blackest he had ever known. Herman had seen his mother swallowed up by violence that he could not understand. He was half dead from fear and trembling with exhaustion. He was starving for a dream to replace the unbearable demands of reality. And mercifully, the healing thrust of his tender psyche, stretched to breaking, did not fail him.

On his first night of separation from his mother, Herman dreamt of home. Everyone was gathered again around the dinner table in Bydgoszcz, safe, laughing and happy. But then, he woke up and came to in the dark. As he lay in bed, encircled in the arms of Isydor, who was trying to be a father to him now, Herman saw a small figure in the dark ghetto hovel. Mamusia sat on his bed and leaned down to kiss him.

"Did you mean what you said that you don't love me?" Herman

asked her.

"I'll always be with you, Herman," she said in the pitch black. "I'll always be with you." Herman could hear his mother's words but there was no way to see her. They were lost.

The next morning, Herman woke up in the bitter cold of the unheated room. He lay for a while watching his misty breath, thinking about last night's dream that was only a dream. Nothing was certain except his next move. He would get up, wash in cold water, and head out for work with his brothers. Who knew if they would come back or not? Mercifully, as he fell in line on the march to Bugaj that morning, shock returned to the edges of his mind and made the world around him seem slightly dreamy and far away.

In the days after the deportations, Herman saw Jewish clean-up crews scouring ghetto buildings, picking them clean of all supplies. Carts were heaped up with mattresses, blankets, suitcases and clothes, any item that could be shipped to Germany and used. The crews had been given strict orders to process and discard everything else. The scavengers tossed their old neighbors' unus-able belongings onto bonfires that were piled high and belching smoke towards brooding heavens. The sky absorbed the destruc-tion and dropped snow to cover the evidence.

On his way through the ghetto to work one day, Herman stooped to pick up a singed and blackened fragment of photo-graph. He uncurled the portrait of a handsome, well-groomed young couple. The woman was in bloom with the most beautiful dreamy eyes and thick dark lashes. The pair was gazing in soft focus towards a happy future. Herman looked around. The remains of abandoned treasures from thousands of obliterated families were burning on unholy bonfires: books, letters, photographs, history and heritage. It was all being reduced to black smoke. Still young, still not so introspective, it did not occur to him that some miles to the east in Treblinka, the owners of these precious belongings, heir-looms, and mementos of an irretrievable past, were being reduced to the very same state.

That night, Herman had a new dream: he saw his mother in the Umschlagplatz. She was ready to board the cattle car, but she seemed calm. Happy. She was holding the hand of a young girl about his age. The girl wore a royal blue dress. She was scrubbed and shining with clean dark glossy hair, fair skin and red lips. The girl and his mother both looked over their shoulders, back to where Herman was trapped at the far end of the siding, and blocked by the crowd. Herman saw his mother hand the girl something. A photograph? The pair examined it. Mamusia was pointing towards him, telling the girl to bring the memento to him. He saw her cup the girl's small pretty face in her hands, kiss her on the forehead, and smile like she was content with the transaction. The girl moved down the platform towards Herman; her eyes fixed on his.

Coming closer, she picked a path through the crowd, weaving in and out of sight. All the chaos and sound faded. Herman saw only the girl in the bright blue dress with laughing eyes as she advanced with a gift from his mother. But suddenly she was gone. Vanished. He looked all around. She was not there. His mother? She was gone too. She had been loaded on the train that was ready to pull out.

Herman scanned faces in the turmoil of the crowd until he spied the girl again and a flash of blue dress as she dashed out of sight. Herman followed, pushing his way through the bodies. Now, he was in the small ghetto but it was deserted. There was the girl ducking into a building. She reappeared in the crumbling doorway that had swallowed her, smiling and flipping her head. Come on. Herman went after her, but he could not catch her as she hurried from building to building through the holes cut into walls. She disappeared again and Herman was alone. He sat on a beat-up, discarded suitcase. Knocking his bony knees together, he rested his chin on his hands. His mother had sent him a keepsake to comfort him. Something special. Told the girl to give it to him, but the pretty thief had made off with his prize.

Soon, numbers in the small ghetto began to swell. Jews who had escaped deportation straggled back in and hid illegally in abandoned buildings, trying to survive cold, illness and starvation. At Dietrich & Fischer, Herman was promoted to running the cross saw. He liked how the noise and thrum of the heavy machine crowded out the unpleasant sounds and sensations, which flashed through his mind when it didn't have anything to fix on.

One day, while the foreman was out of sight, Herman listened to two nearby workers talking. They noticed him tilt his head to listen in, but ignored him. Adults no longer bothered to shield the young from disturbing conversation. Everyone knew that children were not children anymore. They were ancient inside. Brutality had catapulted their young minds and hearts into premature old age. Starved, with hollowed-out faces and ancient eyes, these little slaves were world weary and old beyond their years, strange distortions of childhood.

"The SS are rounding up the old ones and other illegals and shooting them," one man said.

"Where?" the other asked.

"In the synagogue. Or out at the Rakow forest."

Both men leaned further into work. Only work stood between them and destruction. There was no escape. No one was getting away. Everybody knew that now.

That same evening, exhausted after the usual 12-hour work shift, Herman took his place in the caravan of spent workers as they tramped back from the sprawling lumberyard towards the gates and barbed wire fence of the shrunken ghetto. Even when he was completely exhausted and hungry, Herman had learned how to march mindlessly. Don't think. Just put one foot in front of the other. I could walk in my sleep if I had to, he thought tonight as his column tramped along. He stared at the scrawny ankles and feet of the men who marched in front or alongside him. Shoes were a real prized possession. Men would fight over a pair of dilapidated shoes. No shoes, no marching. No marching, no work. No work, no survival. Termination. Some prisoners wore clogs. Others shuffled along, like him in decrepit shoes, ancient and ill fitting, leaking and falling apart. No socks. Feet were always frozen, blue with cold and numb, except for where they burned in the places that were rubbed raw, blistered or covered with chilblains; painful sores caused by the incessant winter freeze.

Herman could operate feet he no longer allowed himself to feel. And as he walked, he put his mind elsewhere, away from every painful step. Away from his body saturated with hunger and his gnawing gut. Away from muscles that spasmed and ached from working, lifting, shifting and sawing. Work that was too much for his still growing and under nourished body to handle. Away from the emotional agony of lost parents.

On this evening, as the marching column of workers neared the synagogue close to the entrance of the small ghetto, Herman heard the commotion before he saw it: rapid bursts of submachine gun fire, the cries of infants, and the terrified screams of women.

"Schnell, schnell." Their guards tried to hustle the workers past the carnage that was coming into view. The man directly behind Herman leaned forward slightly. "Ukrainian guards," he whispered. Herman now saw the soldiers in unfamiliar uniforms aiding the SS in the night's work. Outside the synagogue, a group of women were writhing in anguish. Several had fallen to their knees to rock and wail. Others were collapsed against the synagogue. The shadows of flames from a nearby fire, blazing white hot, were licking the building's walls and dancing across the crumpled bodies of the women.

The Ukrainian guards were rough and deliberate, as they pulled small infants and toddlers from their mothers' arms, unmoved by their agony. There was a rifle butt to the head for any woman who would not let go of her child. Once the baby was snatched, the guard caught it by one leg and swung it against a nearby wall to shatter its skull. Then the small body was tossed into containers that were thrown into the inferno or lobbed directly into the flames. Mothers did not suffer for long. Groups were downed by the submachine guns that the guards had trained on them. Herman heard the bullets ricochet off the synagogue. He saw dead or unconscious women dumped into the containers with the remains of their children.

"Herman, look away." Herman heard Sam, marching beside him, spit the order. But he could not look away. He watched as a Ukrainian guard tossed an infant high into the air and caught it in a wide flat pan. Then the man ran, balancing the child in the pan, who knew if it was dead or alive, and hurled the small body into the flames.

Now, Herman did look away. He felt the familiar and welcome sensation of numbness coming over him. A tingling in his chest. A slowing down of thoughts. The muting of smells and sounds like the earsplitting screams from women driven to madness. The rapid rat tat tat of gun blasts. The roar of flames fed by more human debris. The stench of burning flesh. The whoops and laugher of Ukrainian guards. Like any sport that improves with practice, the soldiers were getting better at their blood sport, becoming more efficient and precise. Herman started to pant. If he could just cry, he thought, it might relieve the strange pressure climbing through his body, squeezing his head. But he could not cry.

That night Isydor perched beside Herman on the bed in the latest miserable room that they now shared. "Herman, try not to think about these awful things," he said.

"Why not?" Herman barely heard his own question.

"Because we are Jews and to be a Jew is to choose life no matter what."

"This is not life." Herman was not threatened by any emotion. I still can't cry he thought. The secret place inside him that produced tears had gone numb like his feet; the leaden hunks of meat at the end of his thin legs.

"We will survive this and make a new life. A good life." Isydor sounded determined.

"Tatus and Mamusia are gone," Herman said. He accepted that his parents no longer shared their hell, he was glad they were spared it. But after the war, if there ever is an end to this, he thought; if there is a single Jew left alive to make a normal life, then without Mamusia and Tatus, life will be unbearable for me. Herman had never looked into the future before, but he saw this now. I love my brothers, but my parents were my life, the ones who protected and cared for me.

"Tatus and Mamusia would want us to fight to live and be together. Be happy." Isydor tapped the side of the mattress. Tap tap. That was all there was to it. Herman lay awake in the dark, exhausted, but unable to sleep. His mind flashed and flickered, lit up with the scenes in front of the synagogue. The crackle of fire in his ears. He tried to squelch each image before it grabbed hold. He stood guard over eruptions from a crowded, volatile memory. Please let me sleep. Let me have a good dream. But when he finally lost consciousness, he just tumbled into darkness. Overloaded, the projector of his mind had ceased to run.

Herman met a friend. His name was Hesiek. He was the same age as Herman but a little smaller. The cross saw that Herman ran at D & F was twice his size. One day a Polish supervisor noticed that he was growing careless from hunger and fatigue. But instead of a beating, he escorted Herman back to the paint shop. Hesiek was there, painting stretchers. Hesiek had been separated from his family during the big deportation. He was alone and fending for himself. That night, Herman pulled his new friend by a sleeve and presented the small, pale boy with the curious eyes to Isydor. "He doesn't have anyone, can he stay with us?" he asked. Isydor nodded. The two boys looked at each other and grinned.

Of all his brothers, Isydor was like a god to Herman. He always felt safe whenever Isydor was around. Because Isydor had been head of the Wolborz Judenrat, it gave him influence with the Jewish police and committee that ran Piotrkow, and he had used it to get his family work at D & F. He couldn't save my parents, my aunt and uncle, Herman thought, but Isydor bought time for the rest of us. The work in Bugaj was backbreaking, but it was better than deportation to Treblinka or a firing squad out in Rakow forest.

And Isydor was a good dentist. The Polish firemen at the camp liked him because he treated them well and cured their toothaches. Maybe he was just a Jew and not really worth their respect, but still, Isydor did have a way of commanding it. He was only 34, but he always seemed very mature and poised. He was optimistic and resourceful like Tatus, but he reminded Herman of Mamusia too; thoughtful and dependable and serious like her. When Isydor looked at people, even the roughest SS man, he seemed to be listening calmly and intently. He was always in control of himself.

Other prisoners often panicked or fell apart, but Isydor stayed cool. He could negotiate for food and favors with a quiet dignity that impressed even determined Jew haters.

Having Hesiek around cheered Herman up. It felt good to have a friend who was the same age and saw the world like he did. But the weight was rolling off Herman's body. The daily ration consisted of just a slice of bread, coffee and thin soup, and it was nowhere near enough calories to fuel his developing body and keep him going. Every day, the boys were forced to march to and from work in the lumberyard and struggle through a 12-hour work shift. It was a grueling regimen for even full-grown men who were strong and well nourished. Herman's bones stuck out and hurt when he fell onto his mattress at night.

Talking or slacking earned a beating with a stick from the Polish firemen who supervised them. Even so, Herman and Hesiek managed to share whispered conversations and diversions. One day, Hesiek pointed at a boy their age who had wandered into the paint shop. The boy's hair was completely white. "See that kid?" Hesiek said, pointing at him. Herman nodded.

"The SS took him with the women, children, and old men that they found hiding in the small ghetto after deportation." Herman looked at the boy who had delivered his message to a foreman and was headed for the door. He seemed closed off and passive. Deadpan. "The SS made them all undress," Hesiek said.

"How many?" Herman interrupted.

"I don't know, a few hundred. They made them all undress in the snow in the woods. SS beat them with bayonets and sticks, and terrorized them with the dogs. Then they machine gunned them so they fell into a big ditch that had been dug." Hesiek went quiet. Herman looked at him and lifted an eyebrow. What did it have to do with the kid? Hesiek suddenly remembered the point of the story. "The kid was there. He was only wounded when he fell in the ditch. They buried him under the bodies and covered them with frozen dirt and leaves. He waited until night and got out."

"I thought he was buried." Herman sounded unconvinced.

"He managed to get out. He climbed over the bodies. He had no clothes, he was naked, but he made it back into town. It made his hair go white. The shock."

Herman touched his own dark hair, still thick despite lousy nutrition. How much shock had he absorbed? Enough to turn his hair white?

"More work less talking." A Polish fireman was prowling the floor and had stopped to give them a tongue-lashing.

Herman and Hesiek tried to do everything together. Work seemed easier when they did it side by side. One day when the freezing weather was finally giving way to warmth and the promise of spring, the two boys were sent to bring sheets of plywood from the yard to the factory. They worked for a while, both sweating, and then sat, out of sight, against a pile of wood, drowsy in the sun. Soon they were sound asleep.

Herman thought that his arm was being yanked from its socket by the enraged fireman, who found them, and dragged the two boys to the Fire Chief's office. He shoved Herman against the wall outside. "Wait here," the fireman snarled. Hesiek was pulled into the office and the door was slammed shut. Soon Herman heard the cries, screams alternating with whimpers. After a few minutes, the door flew open. "You, get in here now," the fireman screamed, shooting spittle from his mean, wet lips. Herman was fixed to the spot. The fireman lunged for him and struck him on the back with a stick to propel him through the door.

"Do it," the Chief yelled at the two Polish Fireman who stood in the room. Herman saw that Hesiek was close by, curled up in a ball on the floor, and motionless.

"Pull down your pants," one fireman ordered.

Herman fumbled and tugged down his threadbare stained pants. They slid over his boney non-existent hips.

"Bend over." The Fire Chief was slapping his stick against his left hand and shifting his weight from one foot to another. But he didn't strike Herman. He nodded to his two subordinates who carried their own sticks. Herman braced himself against a chair and leaned forward. The first blow felt like pure heat, a hot poker against his tender pale skin. There was a pause. Another blow. Searing. And then a deep after-pain that throbbed. His eyes were watering. Not really tears. Some kind of whole-body reaction to the shock. He was trembling inside and out. The firemen struck his bare buttocks twice more, hard. But Herman sensed one of the men hesitating like he hoped each blow would be the last he had to give. He wants to stop, Herman thought. Please God, let him stop. Another blow, and Herman felt the flesh on his buttocks split, as a new level of agony sent his mind into overdrive. He was terrified of being hit again. He needed to run and knew he couldn't.

"He's cut and bleeding," the reluctant beater said.

"Keep going." The Chief was breathing heavy. Herman braced himself but could not control his terror. Could not defend against the pain of the attack on the raw, bleeding meat of his buttocks. He was undone.

"Isn't this one the dentist's kid?" The one fireman half lowered his stick.

"Okay stop," the Fire Chief said. Herman collapsed on the floor and pretended to be passed out. He felt watery vomit rising from his empty shrunken stomach.

"Get 'em out," the Chief said. The firemen lifted Hesiek and Herman to their feet. "Pull up your pants," one said. The fabric against Herman's flesh was unbearable. Both boys were whimpering as the firemen marched them back into the factory.

The SS had transferred all the Jews to D & F from the ghetto, which was now Judenfrein, Jew-free. Their new home was an encampment inside the sprawling lumberyard. This meant less time wasted marching back and forth, more time working for the Nazi war effort. Now they lived in round ten by ten plywood huts that they had built themselves and equipped with a wood burning stove, a table and bunk beds. As many as 20 men squeezed into each small hut. Isydor had secured one for the four brothers, two cousins and one friend--Hesiek. A gang of other workers shared the tight space.

For weeks after the beatings, Isydor tended to Herman's and Hesieks's lacerations and bruises. He bathed, washed, and applied a little stolen ointment so the cuts wouldn't turn septic. Sitting, sleeping and walking were painful, but in time, Herman's wounds healed. And soon they were completely forgotten with the arrival of a powerful new distraction.

One day, back for another stint in the paint department, Herman saw the girl. She looked to be a little younger than he was and she was dressed in an ill-fitting, brown, shapeless dress. The sleeves hung down, almost covering her grubby hands. Herman saw how she grabbed and tugged the edge of each frayed sleeve with curled fingers like she was holding on for safety. He noticed the outline of small breasts, deep brown eyes, and dark, thick hair. Such a beautiful face. She reminded him of his dream girl from Piotrkow. He couldn't stop looking at her. She must have felt his stare because she looked up at him from under her lashes and smiled. Herman was in heaven. He hadn't known that he could feel happiness like this. It took days before he had the courage or the opportunity to whisper hello and ask her name. "Rachel," she said. She curled her fingers around her sleeves and gave them a little tug.

Herman was knocked down by first love. Rachel overran his thoughts: will she be there tomorrow? Will I be able to talk to her? What does she think of me? Does she like the way I look? He thought about touching her. Kissing her. Doing more. His body was filled with amazing sensations. He awoke in the morning aroused and yearning to touch the beautiful girl in the paint shop in all her secret places. Had anyone noticed his erect state? He twisted around in his bunk and scanned the faces of his bunkmates. A few snickered, but nobody said anything.

Thoughts and fantasies of Rachel helped ease Herman's misery. Young first love was awakening in him, filling him with energy that helped him to forget his hunger, exhaustion and fear. But it didn't last long. After only a few weeks, Rachel was gone. Maybe she will come back. Herman craned his neck to look whenever someone came into the paint shop. Everywhere he went around the camp, he scoured faces, looking for Rachel and her beautiful chocolaty eyes, but she had disappeared.

Months went by, every day like the one before. It was always cold, then came the relief of warm weather, and then cold again. Herman lost track of time. He was becoming more depressed. Continual hardship and brutality in the forced-labor camp at Bugaj made for a miserable and shutdown existence. A never-ending cycle of work, beatings, near starvation, and lack of sleep was grinding Herman down into a state of chronic hopelessness.

Chapter Eight
Death Train

There was no warning, there never was. Shock and surprise were key elements in SS brutality. They relished the psychological torture of always refusing to say what would come next. Early one day, the Polish Fire Chief lined up the prisoners at Bugaj and told them that next morning they should be ready to leave. Where? the prisoners wanted to know. Just be ready to leave. That night, Isydor was lighting the stove in their plywood hut. Cold weather was coming on again and the oldest Rosenblat had pedaled his influence to scrounge scraps of wood to feed a small fire and keep them all from freezing.

"Isydor, are we going to Treblinka?" Herman asked. "Are the Germans going to gas us?"

"No Herman, they won't gas us. They are going to try and work us to death, but we are strong. We will keep going won't we?" Isydor smiled and almost looked like he meant what he said.

"Then why are they moving us?"

"Because the Russian and the Allied Forces are getting closer." Scraps of news made its way into the camp. Sometimes just rumors or wishful thinking. Sometimes facts.

The Nazis are on the run?" Herman smiled. It didn't look like they were on the run. They seemed to control things and dole out beatings the same way they always did. "And the Allies and the Russians don't hate the Jews?"

"Not as much as the Nazis hate us." Isydor smiled. "No Herman. They don't hate the Jews. Soon the war will be over and then we will be free. Until then we keep working, okay?" Herman went to sleep oblivious to the dread that was filling his brother in the bunk below. Isydor lay awake most of the night, almost certain that tomorrow they would all be shipped to the gas chambers in Treblinka.

Early next morning, as the workers lined up in the freezing dawn, there was strong tension in the air. A truckload of SS men in green uniforms rolled up full of noise and swagger. They leapt off the truck and the beatings with sticks and rifles began. "Raus, raus!" Herman heard the order to move out and march. One foot in front of the other. He knew how to do it. But today they marched forever. Exhaustion rolled in like the tide and engulfed the column. Herman saw men too spent to go on stop in their tracks, crumple and drop. Others staggered for a while then faltered, lurching forward and leaning at crazy angles. Ankles unsteady, too weak to bear their own weight, they tipped off balance, propelled forward, then fell sprawling in the snow.

Two men ahead in the column tried to drag a friend along, but he fell. Stooping over him, they tried to pull him up by his arms. The man just dangled from his wrists, dead weight, then shook his from head side to side in the snow. No. He could not go on. Herman's row stepped over him. A pistol went off. A sharp retort and a ringing echo in the cold air. An SS had shot him. To fall and not get up was a death sentence. No mercy for the weak and sick.

Once they collapsed, they were ready targets for SS looking to pick off easy victims. Fewer to kill at the other side. One foot in front of the other, but Herman began to stumble. He felt Sam on one side, Abraham on the other. Each brother put a hand under his armpits. They dragged him along.

In the distance, he saw a railroad siding, and cattle cars. Panic spread along the lines. Serious miscalculations had led many men to the wrong conclusion, led them to believe the fairytale that Isydor had told Herman: as long as they worked for the war effort, were of use to the Nazis, could weather the grind and not be crushed by it, then they would live. But here were the cattle cars all lined up and ready for loading. Everyone knew a cattle car was a one-way ride to a death camp.

Herman felt the terror wash over the column. He looked at Isydor. "It will be okay, Herman," Isydor said. Only now did Herman see his brother's bravado crack. He's not certain at all, Herman realized. How could he be? How could Isydor possibly know more than the SS; more than the men who beat and control us and decide from one second to the next who lives and who dies?

"Inside, inside," the SS screamed and crammed the bodies, at least 100 into each car. Not even standing room; one frail specimen packed against another. All the jostling and panic made the growing claustrophobia worse. The men shifted around in the tight space like frightened twitching animals penned in and filled with the impulse to bolt. Herman's car was stuffed to the point of suffocation and then its crush of men was driven back against the rear wall to make room for yet more. From outside came the ranting of SS, the cries of prisoners, clattering of doors, clanging of locks.

Piotrkow had been cleared out completely now, even its factories. All was Judenfrein. Jew free. Women had been marched to the railroad siding also and packed into their own cars. Herman listened to shrieks and goodbyes, the painful separation of husbands from their wives. As he heard the pitiful drama beyond the walls of his new prison, he felt his feelings shifting back and forth: sorrow for the losses all around him, and rage at the Nazis who inflicted them.

A slow dying of sounds. It took forever but the noise of preparation finally ended. Herman felt and heard the coupling of the service engine to the cars. The warm-up blasts of the engine. The train lunged forward, then lurched back. The metal squeal of stiff wheels straining to turn, breaking the inertia and gaining momentum. We are moving, Herman thought. Towards death probably.

It was cold in the car despite the heat from compressed bodies. Barely any light or air came in through the two small barred windows cut high into the wall. Herman was filled again with more panic and claustrophobia. And anger at the other men for crushing him. He took deep breaths, fighting the urge to scream and kick out. Get away from me. Give me room. His face was pressed against the sweaty back of the listless man riding next to him. Still short, still growing, he wasn't tall enough yet to stand head to head with the men plastered against him on every side.

They rode into the night. Leg muscles gave way from standing but there was nowhere to drop. Each exhausted traveler was held upright and in place by the crowd around him; an overgrown congested forest of puny beings. A stench filled the car as human waste from trapped men ran onto the floors. Herman began to cry. No noise, just his shoulders shaking. Abraham was nearby. He snaked his arm and managed to grab and pull him, hoisting him up towards the small window. Herman took gulps of cold air and felt calmer. After a while, his tired arms trembling, Abraham had to drop Herman back into his slot on the floor. He raked his hand across the boy's head, a rough caress to say I'm sorry I can't do more.

I can't go on. I can't go on. I want my mother. Herman couldn't stifle his despair, but he had nowhere to vent it. No one can help me. These grown men can't even save themselves. He fell to his knees, stretched out, wriggling through the forest of legs and ankles until he was somehow lying on the floor. He retched from the smell, but eventually his exhausted mind snuffed out. Herman slept and found his recurring dream: he saw the girl in the blue dress. She was holding the photograph his mother had sent her to give him in the Umschlagplatz. Running and ducking, the girl raced through the tunnel cut into the buildings of the Piotrkow ghetto as Herman chased after her.

Herman woke up, his head awash in the suffocating stench and swill of waste that covered the floor. He didn't care. He listened to the train and its rickety ride. Clickety click. Clickety click. Even and robotic on the tracks but inside the car, Herman heard its human cargo unraveling: quiet moans, prayer, and weeping in the fetid darkness.

He slept again and had another dream, new and amazing. In his dream, Herman opened his eyes and this time he was alone in the velvety darkness of the cattle car, lit only by watery beams from a pale winter moon. His fellow passengers were all gone. He sensed something move in the corner. Squinting, he saw her there, wrapped in dim light and shadow--the girl from Piotrkow. But this time she was not trying to elude him. She stood on one foot, the other one lifted and pressed against the wall, as she leaned back in a pose of utter seduction. Herman, crouched in a primitive gesture of beholding, then stood and made his way towards her. She stretched out her arms to embrace him and he caught her perfume sweetening the stench of the car. She lifted her small face and found his mouth. He parted his lips. She draped her arms around his shoulders and loosely clasped her hands behind his neck. Herman ran his hands up and down her body, played her boney torso with his fingers. Felt her small breasts. She kissed him. He had never kissed a girl before. He felt it in every nerve of his exhausted being. A shudder and vibration. Herman awoke into a dreary dawn. The train had rolled into daylight and was slowing to a stop.

Activity outside. The clatter of the door opening and an icy blast of air like cold water heaved from a bucket. The crush of men expanded outwards to meet the extra space of the opening. "Raus, raus!" They were ordered out. Stiff, aching, legs were trembling. Herman jumped from the car. Now unsupported, dead men fell down. "Bury them!" Those too sick to move were dragged out, thrown down in the snow, and shot. The corpse pile was even higher now. "Bury them!" Herman was assigned to the men cleaning the car. Scoop up excrement and pass it to someone else. Nose held to the side. The waste caked his hands.

All the work finally done, SS set down a bucket of water, and three two-pound loaves for the remaining 70 or so men to share. Herman ate his ration with shit stained hands and retched. Barely any break at all. The door slammed and locked. The screech of wheels. Thirty dead and disposed off. Thank God, there was a little more room now.

Come night, only fitful sleep. Some men stood to pray. Dear God, were they still observant? Herman had learned so little about his religion. He was still unschooled and unfamiliar with Hebrew. The prayers, intoned quietly, sounded like a strange chant as Herman half listened and drifted into reverie. He thought about Rachel and his other dream girl from Piotrkow. The two girls were merging in his mind to become the ideal beauty he longed for. The physical drive towards sex and procreation was still alive in his starved but developing body. Clickety click, the train on tracks, and closer, the murmur of an almost alien tongue forming prayer: Hebrew, the ancient language of the Jews who were doomed to wander. Doomed to die. But somewhere deep inside, Herman was still alive to the world and dreaming of love.

How long did they travel? Days or weeks? One day Herman saw a station sign: Czestocowa. The birthplace, he remembered, of his maternal grandmother. Every day or two, the same drill: the ejection of the dead, execution of the sick, disposal of the corpses. A few times, the obscene site of bodies left above the frozen ground, piled up in the center of a circle of snow stained ruby-red. The same meager loaves of bread tossed in the car with water slopped in a metal bucket. Each of his three brothers tore a corner from their ration and gave it to him—almost a whole extra slice for him. "I don't' want to take it. You don't' have enough to spare." Herman said and looked down.

"Eat, Herman. You are growing," they said. All three brothers were so good and devoted, and showed immeasurable kindness. But it only pained a boy who was now otherwise lost in a world of cruelty.

As always, before they could eat, the riders first had to clean the car, scrape and remove shit with their bare hands. Herman could not stomach it. One day, he leapt down from the car and wiped his hands on the ground, palm then back, palm then back, soiling the white snow. A cracking sound. A shot of agony between his shoulder blades from the rifle butt. He threw back his head and yelped in pain. My back is broken, he thought. He couldn't rise and obey the SS man's command to get back in the car. He waited for the click and bang, but Isydor reached out from the car with both arms and dragged Herman's light and bony frame up and through the opening. Then he gently rolled up his brother's shirt and packed cold snow on the wound. "It's going to be alright, Herman." Herman felt his brother's soft touch trying to soothe the pain. Herman rested against the side of the car, head on his knees. He was in agony. "I just want to die," he murmured.

More stops, and sometimes a chance to go outside, stretch the legs, and exercise a little in the bite of clean, cold air. Or just sit with the door open and look out into the countryside, the fresh air coming in. At one stop, the women's car was uncoupled and sent off down another track to a new fate or to the same fate in a different hell. Cars were added and others unhooked. Careful logistics: the packing up and shipping out of unwanted Jews. Human cargo dispatched to a last destination, a problem to be resolved by a final solution.

Another time, a stop, but then a hurried start again. "The Russians are coming. The Russians are close." The rumor buzzed around the car. Germans on the run with their cargo of Jews? They were down to thirty in Herman's car now. Plenty of room to sit and stretch out. They had designated one corner as a latrine and garbage dump. Herman thought about small mercies: there was more space in the car. And maybe help was on the way. People coming to save them..Maybe hope could live a little while longer.

One day something new. Not just a stop, but a destination. As the crow flies, the men in the transport had traveled about 420 miles. But the journey had seemed endless, a circuitous route, zigzagging on never-ending train tracks. The odd glimpse of a station sign told them that they were in the German countryside. The train pulled into a siding and then nothing. A long wait as late afternoon came on. When it was almost dark, they heard the familiar command to get out: "Raus, raus."

Herman jumped down and looked around at the ashen and exhausted men now lining up. Of the 1000 or so who had first been loaded onto the death train, less than half were staggering off now to form a familiar column, four abreast. Herman fell in line to join the march. With muscles sore and cramping, the prisoners struggled to pick up the pace, and hoof it away from the the railroad station where the train had dropped them. They saw the name--Weimar. They were in central Germany. Once again, they were marched and beaten, with stragglers shot where they fell. Prisoners, convinced that they could not go another step, next made their way uphill, at double time, along some five miles of road that cut through a thick beech wood—Buchenwald.

Chapter Nine
Buchenwald

It was late afternoon and dark, but the camp was lit by the random dance of searchlights. A sign on top of the iron gates read Jedem Das Seine—To Each His Own. Herman mouthed the slogan as he and his cohorts passed through the entrance. Had he known where he was headed, into one of Germany's most notorious prison camps, Herman would have been even more terrified than he already was. As it was, he had no clue where he had ended up. A death camp for sure, he thought, but one that looked as if it went on forever.

Beyond Buchenwald's gates, Herman got his first look at the camp's complex that sprawled over 371 acres. He was yet to learn about the numerous buildings, roads, barracks, SS villas, stables, stone quarry, metal and electronics shops, an infirmary, a brothel, torture chambers, execution rooms, a zoo, a riding barn, a morgue and a crematorium. Buchenwald was like a city--a metropolis devoted to the work of annihilation, to killing it prisoners the long hard way—slave labor, brutality, diseases, starvation and neglect.

As 1944 rolled on and Hitler's military might crumbled under the assault of Allied and Russian armies, Jewish captives began to sense the desperate situation: Nazis, who had wrung almost every ounce of slave labor from the Jews, their criminal classes, undesirables and prisoners of war, were scrambling now to destroy as many of their numbers as possible.

As their enemies advanced on the concentration and forced-labor camps, the Nazis rounded up prisoners for death marches or crammed them in trains to be sent deeper into Germany. They were dispatched, often without food, water or shelter, and in freezing conditions, on journeys that sometimes lasted weeks until they arrived in Buchenwald. Here, for the time being, they were out of reach in the heart of Germany. It pleased the SS to see that many prisoners were dead on arrival or died soon after, collapsing on the march up to the camp from the train.

Men, and women too, poured into Buchenwald. What had been a prisoner count of less than 8,000 in January 1942, had swelled to a bloated 84,000 in Buchenwald by September 1944. Typhus, typhoid and dysentery epidemics were rampant. Sanitation was overloaded and broken down. What little food rations there had been were now exhausted. More and more of the day-to-day running of the camp was given over to inmate groups, to the anti-fascists, and other political prisoners, who wore the red triangle on their prison uniforms. The only thing undiminished in Buchenwald was the SS drive to kill as many Jews as possible before their enemies caught up with them and the war ended.

It was into this madness that Herman arrived as he hovered around his fifteenth birthday. But as he stumbled through the gates into the hell of Buchenwald, one of the first things to catch his attention was a glimpse of beauty: the trees beyond the path where the SS were marching his column were dressed in snow and nearby, in a clearing, Herman spied a glass hothouse. The windows were foggy with condensation but he still caught a flash of deep red, pink and lush green from within--exotic plants carefully cultivated in a field of destruction. Then, in the distance, in bizarre contrast, Herman spotted a tall chimney. A crematorium? Ah it was certain then. They would be gassed.

Herman passed through another double set of gates, topped with two wooden towers. Searchlights and submachine guns were trained on the procession as it lined up in Appellplatz—Roll-Call Square. Beyond, Herman spied what would be his new home--a prison barracks in the overcrowded and infamous Little Camp where the Jews were sardined; sometimes 400 men smashed into a barracks built to house 100.

The new arrivals stood waiting in Appellplatz and Herman watched as 20 men at a time were peeled away from the crowd and led into one of the buildings that bordered the square. Where were they going? His brothers were lined up nearby, but Herman did not dare turn to them with a questioning look.

It began to snow and then to storm. Large freezing flakes covered the shivering men as they struggled to stand motionless in the square like a crowd of broken, emaciated snowmen, too afraid even to shake off the mounting coat of powder. Time dragged. Men fell and were shot. Wolfhounds, barked and howled, as they loped around the square barely restrained by their handlers from attacking prisoners.

Somehow, Herman remained upright, teeth chattering, his flesh turning to ice, and his mind split off from his body. After several hours, it was his turn to move. Walking away from the square, he felt his heart start to piston from inside the chamber of his frozen chest. He saw Isydor and Hesiek. from the corner of his eye. Ah good, at least they are coming too. They passed through the small doorway of a one-story stucco building. Thump, thump, his heart was an engine now.

A tiled room lined with benches and many doors leading off it. Where did they lead? Two doctors in masks. Two guards. An order to strip. Herman dropped his rags on a large filthy pile off to one side. Where were the men who had worn the discarded clothes? Shoulders hunched, he cupped his hands and shielded his genitals. Everything was stripped away now and he was dressed in only his fear. Thump thump. On the table. A cavity search for valuables. His body filthy and stinking, unwashed forever. His masked examiners didn't care. They parted skin, prodded and poked, rough and efficient.

Get up and go through another door. " This way." The guard, shrouded in his thick overcoat, stretched out his arm as a guide-post. A rifle thrown over the other shoulder. "Schnell." Herman's legs were shaking and his heart still pounding--thump thump. The moment was on him. We die as we live, moment by moment.

Beyond the door was another tiled room. On the ceiling were six showerheads. Herman counted them. A boy counts out the things that he finds in the world around him. He waited. Eight men were there, all naked and waiting to die. How many were required in a batch for gassing? he wondered. Cold. Herman's body convulsed, his shivering accelerated by terror. I want to be wrapped in something when I die, he thought. I want to be warm when I die.

Herman saw Hesiek come into the gas chamber and then Isydor, who smiled a weak crooked grin. Isydor will stay with me and help me while I die, he thought. I am so tired. He longed for a cocoon and moved to the corner of the room where he could crouch down. Tightened into a ball, he wedged himself further into the corner. The room was filling up. Chin resting on his scabby knees, he peered up at the other men. All of them were

covering themselves as best they could. Four were praying, standing, rocking. Two there, crouched on the floor, weeping, rocking.
Another one, laughing and rocking. Others were shouting. About
what? At God. Cursing the Nazis. The room was filled with a
grim babble that bounced off the white porcelain walls.

"Herman are you okay?" Isydor was crouching beside him.
Herman tried not to look at his brother's nakedness, the sign of
their utter powerlessness. "We are going to die," he whimpered.

"No if they wanted us dead, we would be dead already," Isydor
spoke with conviction. But Herman was all out of trust. Isydor
does not know. He is not in charge. He does not wear the mask or
the rifle. Herman was so tired; he couldn't keep his eyes open. If I
am going to die, I will die in my sleep. He passed out.

Up, up, now! The guard drove them all up and herded them
through the doorway. Still another room with an SS at a table,
keeping records and doling out Klamemoten: prison uniforms.
The more substantial winter uniforms were long gone, used up
or out of circulation months ago. Only the blue and white stripe
pajamas, paper thin, were left. Just a shirt and pants, no cap or
underpants. Used-up shoes but no socks. Nothing else. It was
Herman's turn in front of the SS man with the paper and pen;
always the same insane bureaucracy. "Name?"

"Herman Rosenblat."

"You are prisoner 94983. How old?" the SS asked.

"Sixteen." He had been sixteen for three years now.

There had been no bathing or delousing but now Herman's
head was shaved, his thick dark hair falling on his shoulders and
onto the floor. Herman looked at the number and the yellow triangle on the sleeve of his shirt and pant leg. He felt the smooth cap
of his skull. Herman Rosenblat died in the shower room. I am
prisoner 94983 now, he thought.

Outside again and snow was coming though the tissue-paper uniform. His ankles were turning over as he stumbled over ruts of frozen mud. "Outhouse." The guard pointed to the stinking outdoor latrine. Inside the barracks, walls were lined with shelves four-deep for sleeping. Herman saw a stove, a couple of tables and three bare bulbs.

"We need six kapos. Volunteers?" an SS barked. Herman watched. Who would have the guts to go first? Him there, the tall one. Now the others stepped forward. They'll get extra food, Herman thought. But they will get extra SS evil eye on them to go with it. Old-timers, not long back from work, stood by the bunks as food arrived: just a lousy slice of black bread and watery soup doled out to the starving men.

"It's all you get," an old-timer said. He had no teeth. "They stopped the morning meal. Food only once a day, at night." It showed. The men in the barracks looked like musulmen—the walking dead. No meat on our bones either. Herman thought about the rocking skeletons in the shower room he had mistaken for a gas chamber. Isydor was eating his bread. He took a final bite, then thrust the last piece towards Herman. No. Herman shook his head. Not tonight. Tonight I feast on being alive, he thought.

Here was Sam coming through the door, and soon after, came Abraham. All four brothers were still together. Where one goes, we all go. Then later, his cousins Barak and Lutek arrived. Half past eight meant lights out. Men rushed to scramble onto the uppermost bunks. At least 100 packed on each of the four wall-length shelves. If one turned, then they would all have to turn like dominoes. Herman collapsed onto a lower bunk with no mattress and was pushed by Abraham against an outer edge. He fell into dark, dreamless sleep, but then came rain. His face was wet. The thin blanket was wet. There was rain coming in. No, it was piss! Running down from the bunks above. Too far to go to the outhouse and too cold. Too hard to push your way back into the bunk after your space had been eaten up by crowded men expanding into the inches that had been yours.

"Tomorrow night, we will be on the top bunk," Sam vowed.

Five thirty and the endless trill of a whistle blown over and over. Herman shuffled in the line for the outhouse, stamping his feet, rubbing his palms, and wrapping his arms around his torso; caught in his own embrace. Teeth chattering in his head, it was hard to breathe.

Roll call. A list of names was shouted and the men ordered to come forward. Pale and shaken, they made their way towards the office of the Roll-Call Officer. They look terrified, Herman thought. Whatever is waiting for those poor wretches can't be good. Every man standing for Appell was trying to hold still, to look inconspicuous. Appointment to a work detail: all four Rosenblat brothers were awarded the stone quarry.

Herman got his first look at the camp in the predawn light. The inmate next to him announced a few landmarks, as they marched, squeezing the words out from the corner of his mouth so the guard wouldn't hear: "Weapons factory on the left. SS infirmary on the right. Beyond that, dog kennels." Herman could hear the barking. "And next to that the execution facility."

The quarry was not far and within the camp confines. It backed up to the sentry line.

Herman found himself paired up with a work mate, Chaim. They were led down into a tunnel and told to load boulders. Chaim was only 35, but he looked 60. "Slow down, kid. Pace yourself. I'll speed it up when I see SS." Herman nodded. They were dumping the rocks into a metal trolley. Impossible to push empty, let alone full.

"This is a death detail, a real Jew killer. Up to eight a day." Chaim sounded rough but Herman knew he was trying to help. " They've been bringing in Italians and Czechs," he said, "but they can't handle it. They're not used to it like us Jews. Don't stand near the edge of the quarry. SS will kick you over the edge. Stay alert. Sometimes they'll force you to push a trolley up the hill to watch it run you down. Or they pelt you with rocks. And be careful whenever you near the sentry line. SS will chase you over the line and the sentries will shoot you for trying to escape."

"What are the rocks for?" Herman hoisted another; it had to be half his weight. He dropped it with a clang in the trolley.

"Who knows? Nothing. Sometimes a road. Just moving rocks around. Another way to kill the Jews?"

"Are they going to gas us?"

"No gassing here. If they want to gas you, I heard they send you over to The Bernburg Sanatorium. Yeah that's where the sick go to convalesce, to the gas chamber in Bernburg. It's like the old bastard Commandant Koch used to say: there are only the dead and healthy in my camp."

"It's not a death camp?" Herman coughed and hacked, trying to clear the dust sticking to his windpipe.

"Sure, it's a death camp. We just die the slow way: work, starvation, illness and torture. If you're lucky, they shoot you. A bullet to the base of the skull. They save that for the Russians they bring in. Like to off those poor bastards straight away. Out in the stable."

"How long have you been here?" Herman asked.

"Forever," Chaim squeezed his lids as though resetting his brain. Under both eyes were deep valleys of blue. His pale skin pulled tight over his skull had a yellowish tinge and was dirty from the swirl of choking dust that filled the tunnel. "SS. Keep working.

No more talk," he whispered.

That night Herman felt like his body had seized up with stiffness and pain. He was crushed against Sam, but at least they had snagged an upper bunk and his brothers had secured him an end again. The lice were back and eating him alive. Herman could not scratch. His arms were pinned close to his sides, his hands caught between his thighs. His only break that day had been an afternoon roll call and then another at 6 PM. Bread and soup followed by lights out.

Mamusia. I can't go on? Please help me. He only mouthed the words. Sometimes he screamed, a silent scream that filled his throat but didn't make a sound. He had been living in muffled despair, among a desperate crowd of men for over two years, since his mother had been taken to Treblinka. Bugaj was agony but easy compared to this.

Herman heard a scuffling in the dark, a sickening thud, and then the sound of a heavy sack being dragged across the floor. The door opened and a cold draft blew through. Herman heard voices: "Push him out, quick."

"Shut the damn door," a man snarled in Yiddish from somewhere in a middle bunk. Herman heard whispers from the doorway, a few grunts, and then the door was closed. He sensed movement across the darkened room, then new scuffling and moans as the renegades tried to wedge themselves back into their crowded bunk.

"Herman, I love you." Mamusia was sitting beside him, her legs dangling from the bunk, her feet swinging a little. Herman could see the glint of her best gold-buckled shoes in the darkness. She stroked his face. Kissed his ear and whispered in it. "I am always with you. I am never going to leave you. I am going to send you an angel to take care of you."

The next morning, Herman braced himself for a trip to the stinking outdoor latrine. It was still dark, the yard lit by electric lamps. As he came out of the barracks, he saw, pushed against the wall, three corpses, frozen solid right where they had been dumped the night before. Were they dead when they were thrown out like garbage? Or were they just too sick and weak to put up a fight against their bunkmates' brutal efforts to help solve the overcrowding problem? Herman looked away from the twisted bodies and their staring eyes. Their shoes had been lifted already.

"You two, take this one to the morgue." Herman glanced at the kapo, standing by one of the corpses, and then he looked away. He can't be talking to me, he thought. "Hey, I'm talking to you, Dumb Kopf!" the man yelled.

"Me?" Herman squinted at the kapo who came at him with his stick. Herman swerved away from the blow, but it nicked his elbow.

"I said you two grab that one now and take him." The kapo pointed to the most mangled remains. Herman and the man in line behind him approached the body. Herman moved for the feet. Not heavy, but awkward. He grabbed the ankles, thin as chicken bones. The two lifted the body and shuffled with it, crabbing along. Herman's helpmate seemed to know where they were going. He steered Herman in the direction of the morgue in the crematorium beyond Appellplatz. It was hard to keep a grip on the dead man's legs.

Herman was only 15, but already he had seen his share of death. Still, he was unprepared for what he found inside the morgue: corpses were neatly stacked at the far end. Two men were loading bodies off the pile into an elevator that descended to the crematorium where attendants fed the fires with skeletal remains; sometimes two at a time. Herman stared at the pile. He saw that the head of one body rested on the feet of the one below him. Piled top to tail in organized strata, the tightly packed bodies were less likely to topple.

"Down there." His fellow pallbearer jutted out his chin, directing Herman to unload their cargo near the corpse stack. Herman was poised to rest the lower end that was his charge to the ground as his helper dropped his top end like a sack of potatoes. The loud crack made Herman flinch as he set down the feet. His eyes blurred and he felt faint. He had been too focused on his task when he first came in to notice what he saw now as he straightened up: three bodies strangled with rope looped around their necks and suspended from hooks that were screwed into the wall.

"Come on, let's go," his partner said like he knew why it was not wise to linger. Herman glanced again at the dangling bodies: two men and one woman. He saw the glint on her foot. She wore only one shoe decorated with a gold buckle. It glinted as he moved to pass by her, his face turned away, afraid to let his eyes travel the length of her body to her face. Herman kept heading for the door, then panic froze him up.

"Come on, let's go," his partner snarled. Herman knew what he would see if he turned around and he was terrified. But he had to look back. Had to make sure it was she. He turned to face the strangled corpses. There was no woman. Just three men draped in blue and white striped uniforms; their bare feet dangling only inches above the ground. Herman saw now that hooks, screwed into the wall at almost equal intervals, ringed the room. He began to count. A boy will count out the things that he finds in his world. "There are 48," the man said as he pushed Herman through the door outside and in the direction of Appellplatz.

Herman discovered that on Sundays most prisoners only worked until noon, unless you were put on the punishment detail and then you worked a full day or did special exercises. The SS made you run double time up a mountain of stone ships and then forced you to slide back down on your belly so that the skin was scraped off your face and hands. Sometimes there was calisthenics and running double time with rocks that SS picked out just for you.

It was always cold outside. Perpetual winter. Buchenwald, Herman learned, sat on the Ettysberg mountain range, more than 1,500 feet above sea level. A perfectly hostile place for the Nazis to house the ones they hated. Eight months of winter and extreme fluctuations in temperature. Inside the overcrowded barracks, it was always bedlam, with fights over food breaking out, and the endless settling of scores. Herman had learned that the barracks nearby housed a band of Danish policemen. Two thousand had been deported from Denmark to Buchenwald after the Danes refused to cooperate with the Nazis.

One Sunday afternoon, a Danish policeman approached Herman and struck up a conversation as they loitered outside their barracks. Herman thought that the Dane did not seem as withdrawn as most of the prisoners he had been watching for the last hour. The majority was like Chaim: musulmen—skeletons that walked. At first the conversation was a little stilted and in German. The Dane spoke it fairly well. German was a second tongue for Herman who had lived in Bydgoszcz where almost half the population had been Volkedeutsch.

"Are there Jews in Denmark?" Herman asked once their conversation had settled into a comfortable vein.

"Of course there are," the policeman said. "But our king refused to round them up and turn them over to the SS. We stand by our Jewish countrymen." The Dane announced this with some pride. Just a few years earlier, Herman had found it impossible to believe that anyone could hate Jews just for being Jews. Now, he found it impossible to believe that there was anywhere in Europe where Jews were not hounded and despised. He thought of Palestine. The home so many Jews longed for. In Bydgoszcz, he and Sam had joined a Zionist youth organization. It was fun at the time, but it didn't really mean anything to him back then. Nowadays, he dreamed of sailing to Palestine, to a Jewish homeland, away from the sickness of the Nazis and all the Poles and Ukrainians who helped them to destroy the Jewish people. "How many prisoners are in this camp?" Herman asked.

"Tens of thousands," the Dane said. "Everyone that the Nazis hate or who won't bow to them."

"Not just Jews?" Herman had seen prisoners who were not Jews, but he thought they were a minority.

"There are political prisoners who oppose the Nazis," the Dane said. "They wear a red triangle. Green triangles are your criminals. There are Allied prisoners of war. They are taking it hard being here. Pink triangles are your homosexuals. Browns are your gypsies. Blacks are your anti-socials or race violators. Purple are your Jehovah's witnesses. Jews, of course, wear a yellow triangle." He pointed to Herman's sleeve.

Herman realized that the Dane was describing the so-called bad elements that his father had told him about when he had been trying to understand the seeds of the nightmare that was now in full swing. They were the ones that Hitler wanted to clear out so that the German people would think he was a great leader. "Hitler hates a lot of people," Herman said to the Dane.

"He certainly does. Pretty soon, there will be more people in here than out there." The Dane pulled his sleeve across his red, runny nose. "And God help anyone who passes through the gates into this place."

Herman could tell that the Danish Policeman was tough. He was underfed of course, but he looked tall and strong. Still he seemed to be trembling a little. "I've seen and heard things in here, no one would ever believe me. I wouldn't believe me," he said now. Herman was hunched over in the cold, his elbows squeezed into his boney ribs. He just looked at the Dane. "That bitch Elsa Koch? he went on, "that's what they called her: the bitch of Buchenwald. They say she had corpses and live men skinned so she could make lampshades from human skin. She liked tattooed skin best and Jew skin."

"Is that true?" Herman wrinkled his forehead.

"They say it is. She had that riding barn built so she could ride her horse inside it for 15 minutes every morning while a damn band played for her."

"Does she still ride?" Herman tried to picture the oddity of a German woman riding to the accompaniment of a band while thousands of starving prisoners suffered and died just outside.

"They kicked Koch and his wife out," the Dane said. "Had them replaced. They're all bastards. The SS experiment on prisoners. Cut them open while they are still awake. Infect them with typhus so they can work on a vaccine. Seal them up in the dark over in the cellblock. Leave them lying there in water and sewage with nothing to eat and drink. They are black when they come out, if they come out." The Dane looked up from the snowy ground where he seemed to see the horrors he was describing. "How old are you kid?"

"Sixteen." The usual lie.

"You're too young to hear about this." The Dane looked uneasy and confused. He stared into Herman's face as though he might find a boy there, but there was no boy left. The Dane saw an old man looking back at him from Herman's eyes. "Well, you're here aren't you? They haven't spared you the sights." The Dane patted Herman's shoulder and then looked around for something else to talk about. "The war is not going too well for the Nazis, kid. They've wasted too much time and energy trying to murder Yids and undesirables," he said after a while. "Got to pick your battles. Can't fight on every front." Herman nodded like he understood. Was pretty sure he did. He was getting older, 15 now. His brothers still protected him when they could, but Herman knew how it went.

"The Allies are coming," the Dane said, "so the bully boys have got their work cut out to try and finish off this lot in here before it's all over. They either do it fast or they are going to have to send us onto someplace where their brethren can finish the job."

The words of the Danish policeman proved prophetic. Within days, the Nazis were again ready to drive more of their human cattle beyond the reach of advancing enemies. From 1937 to 1945, more than 250,000 lost souls, prisoners of all stripes and natioalities, passed through the gates of Buchenwald. Most perished, but Herman Rosenblat was not among the lost. There was new work waiting for the Rosenblat brothers, at the end of another long train ride.

Chapter Ten
Rabbi

"Whenever you have troubles, go see a rabbi," Mamusia said. "The rabbi knows everything. He knows about God, he knows about people. He knows." Herman's mother tapped her spoon on the edge of the pot she was stirring to emphasize her point.

"Mamusia, I don't have troubles," Herman said. They were standing in the kitchen of the apartment in Bydgoszcz. His mother came towards him. She wrapped her arms around his head and pressed it to her breast, holding the sticky spoon away from him. She was warm and she smelled good—like home and the delicious food she was always making; her own special mother smell. "That's right, my treasure, you do not, and may you never have troubles." She gave him a squeeze, released him, and went back to stirring. Herman wished she had cuddled him longer. She was always busy. Now and again she delighted him with these unexpected cuddles and kisses, but they didn't last long. He would have liked more.

How old had he been? Herman tried to think now, when his mother had told him that he should always find a rabbi to help him if he had troubles? Maybe eight? He had remembered the advice after Roma got depressed again a few years back. She had seen a psychologist for a while, but Medicare didn't want to pay for the sessions. Anyway, who knew if it helped? After the latest troubles with his book, Herman had gone to his rabbi who had a solution. "I'm going to recommend Roma see my colleague, Rabbi Oberman. He is a psychologist and a rabbi," he said. Ah, Herman thought, a rabbi who is a psychologist. Perfect!

Now Herman was in Rabbi Oberman's waiting room while Roma was in her session with the Rabbi. Every week for the last three weeks, Herman had brought her to the Rabbi's house where he kept his offices, just a few miles away from where they lived in North Miami Beach. Herman always stayed in the waiting room until her appointment was over and then he drove Roma home.

The door opened and Roma came out. Herman was happy to see her smiling. Whatever he was saying to her, the Rabbi was making Roma feel better, lifting her out of the depression that came on her now and then and had struck again in the last few weeks because of all the book trouble.

"Herman, may I see you for a moment." Rabbi Oberman opened the door wide so Herman could go in as Roma came out. He gestured for Herman to sit on the green cloth couch.

"Herman, I want you to come and see me a few times," the Rabbi said without preamble.

"Why? Roma is depressed not me." Herman smiled wistfully.

"Agreed. But I know that this is a difficult time for you too—all the controversy and the upset about the book."

"I don't let things bother me. I stay positive. I put my mind on good things. How else do you think I survived?" Herman raised his brows. The Rabbi smiled. "I see that. You have a very positive attitude, which is definitely one of the secrets to a long life. But I want to help you so you can help Roma."

Herman thought for a while. It hadn't been easy for his wife. She had suffered as a child in the war. Gone through her own trauma, different than his, but still terrifying, especially for a girl. Their life together had been happy but a struggle to make ends meet. She had worked hard as a wife and a mother and a nurse; given a lot of herself to him and their two children. Then there had been the robbery and the shooting that had put their son, Kenneth, in a wheelchair. That really broke her heart. And now all this upset about his book. He stood up and smiled at the Rabbi. "I'll do anything to help Roma."

"Good, then come and see me next Thursday at 11 o'clock," the Rabbi said and showed Herman out.

The appointments with the Rabbi? It was really just talking, Herman decided, but he liked to talk, to tell his stories. He enjoyed people, appreciated the contact. The Rabbi was kind and smart, his new patient could tell.

"Herman, you seem to dream all the time about your mother?" the Rabbi said one day.

"Oh yes I do," Herman said. My mother is always with me. She has never left me. She always watched over me. She still watches over me. A few days ago I was feeling pretty bad. Lots of people saying nasty things, you know?" The Rabbi nodded. "Well my mother came to me in a dream. Shall I tell you?" The Rabbi nodded again. "In my dream, I go into a room and as I look around, I see all my brothers and sister. There is Isydor, Abraham, Sam and Eva, and they are all dancing. There is beautiful music playing. I watch them dance. Such a beautiful feeling. In my dream, I am so happy. Then I look at the doorway and there I see my mother. She is smiling and nodding her head. She is overjoyed that her family is all together again, dancing."

"What does the dream mean?" the Rabbi asked.

"It means that my mother is reminding me not to be discouraged. All the love is still there between me and my brothers and my parents. It never goes away. Even the Nazis couldn't kill it. Even the greatest evil in the world could not kill the love of my family and afterwards my love for Roma. Do you understand?"

"I do," the Rabbi said, "and I am happy for you that you experienced such great love. But how did you feel when your mother was sent away to Treblinka?"

Herman was quiet. His eyes trailed around the room, taking in the spare neatness of the Rabbi's office. He stirred and gathered up the painful thoughts that were silent now and settled into the sediment of his mind. "I felt very bad," he said finally. "What hurt me the most, what I didn't understand at first, was why she told me to get away from her; that she didn't love me no more. I was only 13. For a long time I didn't really know. Then one day in Bugaj, I asked Isydor."

"What did he say?" The Rabbi almost whispered his question so he wouldn't chase away Herman's fragile recollections.

"He said that mother said what she did to save me. She knew I would die if I went with her to Treblinka. She wanted to shock me so I would go with my brothers. She said it to save my life, but it still hurt me very bad." Herman recited his explanation like a lesson he had memorized and tucked away in the library of his mind.

"When did you start dreaming about your mother?" the Rabbi asked.

"Straightaway, right after the SS took her away. At first I wanted to believe that she didn't die in Treblinka that it was just a work camp. But I knew really that she couldn't be alive. Treblinka was a finishing camp. No hope. You know a mother loves her children so much that she will find any way she can to take care of them. That's why my mother came in my dreams. I know that she watches over me."

"I think she does watch over you, Herman," the Rabbi said. "Many people who have gone through similar childhood traumas as you have experience this. They find their loved ones in a new way. They keep them alive inside and truthfully that can feel just as real as meeting them out there in the real world. This is a secret that grieving children often learn that adults do not. They keep their connection and their bond with their lost parent. They keep tight hold of the love inside and it never dies. They learn to talk with their loved ones and keep a relationship." The Rabbi looked at Herman's face to see if the old man's heart was writing anything there.

"That's right." Herman smiled. "That's why I never worry, even when bad things happen. My mother told me in dreams during the war that she would send an angel to watch over me in the camps and she did. I'm still here aren't I? People worry about this thing and that, but I don't worry. We don't see everything. We can't see everything. Even things that seem bad at the time can turn out good, you know?"

"A self-fulfilling prophecy," the Rabbi said and smiled.

"No, it is my mother watching over me." Herman corrected him.

Chapter Eleven
Schlieben

After Buchenwald came Schlieben, and in Schlieben, Herman discovered musulmen with a twist: skeletal prisoners who had yellow skin and eyes that bugged out. Yosek, a German Jew, who had been in the camp for about six months, was training Herman on how to make the Panzer Faust: a German anti-tank weapon like a bazooka. Yosek said it was the chemicals that did it--turned the skin yellow. It was the sulfur and the plastics and the rest of the shit that prisoners had to stir in massive cauldrons and then pour into the three-foot tubes to propel the missiles.

"The chemicals will kill you, without a doubt," Yosek said. He was showing Herman how to assemble the trigger mechanism as they stood at a long primitive table under a canvas roof. This makeshift work area had been created and then held over after the factory had blown up a few months back. Yosek whispered that the SS suspected that the prisoners had done it. Over 100 prisoners had been killed in the blast and who knew how many more in the SS reprisals that followed.

Making triggers was the perfect job for a kid with smaller hands. That's why Hesiek was here too. "The chemicals make you bleed inside and then you die," Yosek said casually. "You can't get away from it, it's in the air. Workers drop like flies. Five a day or more. The German gentiles who handle the stuff wear masks, but of course, they want to keep those bastards alive."

Schlieben was a sub-camp of Buchenwald, about 150 miles away, not far from Leipzig in Elbe Ester. Herman's transport had arrived by train. It took days to get there. The train had sat in sidings during the day and rolled mostly at night; they guessed it was to avoid the Allied bombs. The raids were in full swing now, day and night. Herman saw it as a lost opportunity, their train not getting bombed. Better to buy it from a friendly bomb than from a slow chemical death.

The camp was massive, nearly a thousand acres, but sparsely populated compared with Buchenwald: just a few thousand prisoners here. Mostly Polish Jews shipped in from Krakow and the slave-labor camp at Skarzysko-Kammiena via Buchenwald There were gypsy women and French women from Ravensbruck, a women's concentration camps. Hungarian Jews too brought in from Budapest. "They're not real Jews." Yosek said and shook his head like an authority. "They don't speak Yiddish and they are Hungarians first and Jews second. So where were their Hungarian friends when the Nazis were rounding them up to die in a vat of chemicals?"

Just as Herman had worked for the Nazi War effort in Dietrich & Fischer woodworking at Bugaj, he was now working for the Fatherland again at Schlieben under the auspices of the HASAG munitions plant. "HASAG is Hugo Schneider Aktoemgesselschaft-Metalwarenfabrik in case you care," Yosek had said. Herman didn't care. Yosek was right about the fumes, though. They were noxious. You could taste them wherever you went. Herman could feel his lungs and whatever living tissue he had left shriveling up.

German Jews trained the new workers, kapos helped supervise, and the overseers were SS Masters. The younger SS were the most brutal Herman had encountered so far and after Buchenwald that was saying something. Food was kaput and the black market for food out of control. The only good thing? Better bunks. Just one or two men up and down. A mattress and pillow filled with wood shavings and no middle-of-the-night waterfall of piss. But the lice, as usual, were everywhere; the barracks were crawling with them. Herman's flesh was a trellis of scratches and scabs that he clawed with filthy nails. Typhus was definitely in the cards for him if the chemicals didn't get him first. Either way he was a goner. No one was getting out of Schlieben alive.

It was December 1944. For the first time in over two years, Herman was on a different work detail than his three brothers. They were on the nightshift in the chemical foundry, the geiserei, in a section of the factory built out in the woods. They were up close with the poisons, stirring and cooking them all night. Sam had it the best. He was on a detail that got to work out in the fresh air some of the time. They brought the chemical powders from storage to the yellow-skinned workers who turned them into the poison brew that they mixed in cauldrons and then poured into the missiles. There was one bonus reserved for these unfortunate slaves, Herman found out. They called it giftesoup or poison soup. A thin mixture fed to the men on the nightshift in the foundry in hopes it would keep them alive and working longer.

Soon, Herman was moved from the trigger assembly in the outdoor tent to the cinderpakraum. This was a workshop where the boys sat alongside German women who were volunteers for the war effort. It was warmer here. They were permitted to sit and the work of assembling detonators or packing boxes was easy.

Herman worked the 5 AM to 6 PM shift. Every morning and evening before and after work he tried to catch a moment with his brothers as they knocked off from the nightshift. Herman looked for them as they staggered out of the woods and back to the men's barracks where they were housed.

"Herman, Herman, come here." One of the three would call him over when SS weren't watching. "We saved you some soup." A couple of spoonfuls in the bottom of a tin cup. Herman drained it. He was existing on one small slice of bread a day and a cup of water. Not even. Sometimes there were no rations. After years of starvation, his body was giving out. Chronic headaches and stomachaches. Blurred vision. Boils and infected sores from the lice. His brothers looked like they were in worse shape, but at 1AM when they got their soup ration, they managed to siphon off a drizzle for him. Sometimes Sam was in charge of dishing it out to the nightshift and he managed to hold back an extra spoonful for his little brother. Herman wondered how they did it. Where did they get the discipline to keep from gulping down the little food they had been given and saying Herman can fend for himself now?

Some of the German women in the cinderpakraum had a heart. When they could, they gave the Jewish kids working alongside them food scraps. Every crumb helped a poisoned, ailing body that was screaming for food and ready to drop from hunger. One day, working on the line, Herman felt the lice eating him alive. He slid his hand under his shirt and scratched and clawed until his belly and chest were raw. The German woman opposite was eyeing him and scowling. After a while, she pushed back her chair, got up and walked over to the SS Master. Herman saw her talking and pointing in his direction. Panic ignited in him. He was infested with lice and he bet a few had jumped ship onto the good Frau. He had seen kids beaten to a pulp for less: for dropping a carton of detonators or not lifting boxes fast enough. The woman came walking back towards him. The SS Master remained where he was, unperturbed, and looking in another direction. The woman stood over Herman as he cringed. He looked down at her feet. She wasn't fat, but her legs seemed large and deformed; the flesh of her ankles somehow spilling over the edges of her sturdy brown shoes.

"I told him that you and the other boys need a good shower at least once a week," she said. "He said to see him after the shift." She smiled at Herman who nodded his head. His bet was that he was going to get a good beating not a tubbing. But that night, the kapo hustled him and a group of boys into the shower. "And don't get out until every louse is gone," the kapo yelled and smacked the last one in line on the back of his head.

Herman stood shivering under the cold stream of water. What was the point? The lice rained down on them from the barrack's ceiling while they were sleeping. I'll be host to a full house by tomorrow morning, he grumbled to himself. He grew used to the cold water and let it flow over his wrecked and ruined young body. Not an ounce of fat on him and his scabbed and scarred skin looked waxy. Knees like ugly knotty protrusions jutted out from his emaciated legs. He walked his stained fingers over the ridges of his ribs and up his boney breastbone. He was battered and bruised. His body, like his life, had shrunk almost to nothing. All that was left were hunger, pain, fear and cold.

Suddenly, it was as though his will to keep on going was leaking out and running down the drain with the water. I can't go on, he thought, and slid under the weight of the realization, down into the corner and out of the path of the weak shower stream, his knees pulled up to his chin. He thought about his first night in Buchenwald. He'd been convinced he was going to die in the shower room he thought was a gas chamber. He wished he had died. Better still, he wished he had gone with his mother to Treblinka. She would have wrapped her soft arms around him and pulled him against her, into her warmth and her own special smell, and they would have expired together. A few minutes of agony and then sleep, forever, and together. Herman was in pain but he couldn't cry. He started to shiver, scrunched up on the hard floor, his teeth tapping together. Cold was constant. He knew he would never be warm again. He turned off the water and wiped himself with the small, threadbare square of towel, then put on his dirty clothes. The same filthy blue and white stripes from Buchenwald.

Out of sight, behind a tree, Herman stood with his brothers now. He tipped his head far back to drain every last drop of soup they had given him, then he wiped his mouth and handed the metal cup to Isydor who took his arm. "Herman, I've arranged to have you transferred to the foundry to work with us."

"Why?" Herman had wanted to be with his brothers, had argued to be in the same work detail, but they had insisted it was too dangerous. He should go in the cinderpakraum where it was warm and safer. Why switch now? Isydor eyed an SS Master in the distance, a small hunchback who was a beast. He made every man, woman and child he could lay his hands on in Schlieben pay for his deformity. There was no end to his rage and he channeled it through his stick when he beat prisoners to death for nothing, for no reason, for any made-up transgression he could concoct. Back in October, Isydor knew, the factory had blown up and killed at least 100 workers. Sabotage probably. Not so hard with all the explosives lying around. A unit of young SS from Altenburg had been shipped in to oversee punishment and supervise the rapid reconstruction of factory buildings. They drove the prisoners night and day until the main factory was almost rebuilt in just six weeks. But the death toll was massive. The SS worked the prisoners to the point of collapse or they kicked them to death. All that zeal, energy and hatred, they had to put it somewhere. Most of the young guns were gone now, shipped off to the front. Conditions had normalized with the older SS guard back in charge. But the hunchback, he was a bastard. "I heard rumors that the SS are going to move us out," Isydor said, focusing on Herman again.

"Where?" Herman asked.

"I don't know, but it's better if you are with us. That way we won't get separated."

"I thought you didn't want me working too near the chemicals," Herman said.

"I don't, but I'm worried that if we are not all together when it's time to ship out, they will split us up. Besides, you will get the soup and you won't be working in the foundry for long. Now go." Isydor gave him a small push.

Never ever discuss the subject of sabotage, Isydor had warned Herman. Don't even say the word sabotage. Why? Because it could get you killed. It enraged the SS that prisoners, either deliberately or through incompetence, were sabotaging the Panzer Faust. Just a touch too little propellant would turn the weapon into a dud. Somewhere on the battlefield, a German soldier fixed on a target, hoisted the weapon, pulled the trigger and nothing. At the factory, the SS would spot check missiles and if they didn't work, they would grab a handful of workers drag them to the Appellplatz and either hang them there or shoot them.

One day, not long after Herman had joined his brothers at the geiserei, he heard the order for all prisoners to gather in the Appellplatz. An unscheduled assembly? That can't be good. Once in the square, Herman stood in a clutch with his brothers. They were waived to one side into a gang of about 100 men. He watched the Camp Commandant enter Appellplatz and stand before a pile of boxes packed with Panzer Faust. Feet apart, hands behind his back, upright in his immaculate black uniform, he surveyed the rows of broken-down prisoners. "I am going to test three weapons. If any of them fail to work, these men will die," the Commandant said and gestured towards Herman and his group. SS faced them, submachine guns at the ready. The Commandant nodded at an SS man, who removed a weapon from its crate, put it to his shoulder and fired. The missile exploded. He selected a second weapon and then a third. They both fired. Herman felt the men around him shuffle and let down as the tension dispersed a little. They all worked. What a miracle. Wait. The Commandant signaled for another to be launched. Element of surprise. Never let them know what's coming next. The SS pulled the trigger and the Panzer Faust fired. The prisoners stared at the Commandant. He might just shoot us anyway, Herman thought. "You had better pray that there are no more complaints from the front," the Commandant said and then he turned and strode out of Appellplatz.

That night in the barracks, Herman was lying on a bunk when he heard a scuffle and shouting from a group of prisoners who had cornered a Jewish kapo by the wall near the barrack's door. Herman knew the kapo. He had been hated at Buchenwald for ratting men out to the SS and stealing food from those too sick to guard their ration. Two men had him pinned. "What have you been saying to the SS?" one of them snarled.

"Nothing," the kapo whined.

"I see you talking to the hunchback bastard," his interrogator yelled. "You told him we were shorting the mixture. That's why the test today." The small prisoner looked barely strong enough to stand, but he held the kapo down and kicked him.

"Lie down, Herman," Abraham warned, but Herman kept

peeking over the side of his bunk. He now saw two men kicking the kapo, who was curled up like a small feral animal against the wall, his fists shielding his head the best he could. The furious prisoners kicked at him for a long time, while he pleaded for them to stop. Herman felt sorry for him. He tried to think of the poor prisoners that the kapo had bullied or betrayed. He deserved his beating, but Herman still felt pity.

The kapo was crying like a kid: "Please don't hurt me." A group of men pulled him to his feet and jostled him towards the door. The kapo knew what was coming. He leaned back, stiffened his legs, and dug his heels into the floor. Others came to help dislodge him. They took hold of his arms and legs and carried him like a chair. Someone held open the barrack's door and the others hurled the kapo as far into the yard as they could, then slammed the door and leaned against it so he couldn't come back in. Herman heard a rapid burst of gunfire and the men moved away from the door. No one opened it to look outside.

For a few days, spring was in the air. The snow was melting. Best of all, Allied air raids were on the increase. Herman heard the planes fly over them at night en route for their strategic targets: productions facilities, major cities, highways and bridges. He recognized the distinctive sound of their engines. The prisoners exchanged smiles and felt a small excitement. Just what if the Allies came and rescued them before they all dropped dead in this hellhole?

At work in the forest, Herman would see the night sky light up as bombs dropped and distant fires blazed. A few times, Schlieben had been hit but not since Herman had arrived. When the air raid sirens sounded, the SS took off and left the prisoners alone to fend for themselves during the danger. Then the prisoners would wander unsupervised into the cool night air and listen to the fireworks of destruction going off in the distance. The flares were like messages of hope. Hold on a bit longer they seemed to say. Drag yourself through another night of misery; help is on the way.

Herman had listened to the women in the cinderpakraum fret about the advancing enemy armies. The one with the fat feet who had got him the shower told him that she was worried sick about what the Russians or the English would do to German citizens if they won the war. She couldn't imagine life under an enemy regime. Herman listened and scratched his fleabites.

Change was in the air. The SS were distracted. They drove prisoners to step up the work. The insane screaming to go faster, faster was what terrorized workers the most. But despite this, there was a feeling inside the camp that it was all unraveling. The tide was beginning to turn.

A power supply blew up and the electric fence went out. It was not uncommon to see men who had killed themselves by running at the fence. They hung there, fried, until their bodies were taken down; their attempt to end it all a success. Now the fence just penned them all in with the juice sputtering on and off until the electrical workers could get it fixed and keep it fixed. As usual, soldiers with guns stood guard in watchtowers at intervals along the fence and extra soldiers in special blue uniforms were brought in to patrol the perimeter. Anyone trying to get near it was shot. But there were blind spots in the fence and days when the patrol guards were fewer than usual.

Now that Herman was working the night shift, he enjoyed an unfamiliar luxury: strolling the barracks area after he finished work in the morning before he headed to his bunk for sleep. Confined to the compound, prisoners on the night shift could enjoy some peace and quiet while the day laborers worked their shift. The SS were away in the sprawl of factory buildings driving productivity. Faster,

faster, faster, it was always the same.

When Herman had worked in the cinderpakraum, the German women had sometimes let him or one of the other boys go to the kitchen to bring back coffee for them. They knew that the boys scavenged for food while they were there, for old vegetable peelings, and stale or moldy bread, but they turned a blind eye.

Now, Herman sometimes risked a walk in the mornings by the garbage bins to look for scraps. One day, after he had passed by the kitchen, he ventured further on his walk. After a while, he found himself dangerously close to the fence. All seemed quiet and it calmed him to look through the wire at the trees beyond. It reminded him that there was a world out there away from the destruction of the camp.

Herman thought of Brazil and felt sure that the people in Brazil were not at war. If things had turned out differently, we could all be there now, he thought. All of us together with Tatus and Mamusia. Only hearing about the war a world away and not suffering through it. He thought about Eva. France was occupied by the Nazis now, was she safe? Did she run away to Brazil or to Palestine? He knew that there were concentration camps for women; one was called Ravensbruck. There were French women from Ravensbruck here in Schlieben. Herman let his mind wander. He put it elsewhere beyond the here-and-now and the painful what-ifs. Herman focused on a single barb on the wire fence. He stared at the spiky knot, thinking about how it could tear his flesh. He stared until everything around it blurred out of focus and took on the feeling of being not quite real.

Beyond the barbed wire, at the tree line, a few yards beyond, Herman detected movement, then he saw her, a young girl, bundled up in warm clothes, her thick dark hair hanging beneath a beret. She stood in the shadow of a tree and looked at him. At least he thought she was looking at him. Herman glanced all around. It was quiet. He watched the girl watching him. He saw her pull something from her pocket. An apple? She squinted, gauging the distance between them, swung her arm in a few practice throws, then hurled the apple with a force that surprised him. The fruit flew across most of the distance between them before it dropped to the ground, rolled under the fence and landed just inches beyond the wire on Herman's side. He looked down at it, a small red and green round on the thin layer of snow that was almost melted in places.

He eyed the girl, who cocked her head. What are you going to do? Herman raised himself up on the balls of his feet. Up then down. Up then down. Go get it. The impulse rose and grew in him. It overpowered his sense of danger, his fear of what might happen if a watching guard saw him and raised his gun to kill. The impulse shunted aside his caution and he sprinted the few yards to the fence, swooped down, snatched up the apple and darted back to his place. A guard must have seen me, he thought, then he waited, panting. Nothing. No shot. No yell. No sound of running feet. He looked out. The girl was gone. In his hand--a small apple. He pressed the fruit to his nose and inhaled the sweetness of its fragrance, then tucked it under its shirt and hurried back towards the barracks.

Herman tried to return to the same spot every day for four days. It wasn't just the lure of the girl and her edible gift, it was the thought that he had cheated death. In the dash to fetch the apple, he had felt alive, free in a strange way, in control of his destiny. Every day for three days, the guards in blue uniforms were on constant patrol. Herman kept his distance. On the fourth day, it was quiet again. He inched towards the fence, not too close, and waited. Not for long. There she was at the tree line, smiling. She threw the apple; the same forceful under-arm swing and her gift rolled under the fence, even closer to him this time.

He faced down his fear; dash and grab then back to safety. He watched the back of the girl's dark coat disappearing into the trees again. Who was she? Was she German? She looked well cared for? Did she belong to one of the women who volunteered at the camp? If so, then why was she on the outside? Did she live in the wood? Near it? He wondered where she was getting the apples. It wasn't even spring yet. Later, Herman saw Yosek. "Could someone get apples around here?" he asked him casually

"Sure." Yosek smirked. "Wander over to the kitchen. Tell them Yosek sent you and they'll give you an apple and a nice juicy sausage."

"Not in the camp, outside?" Herman said. "Can people get apples?" Yosek thought for a moment. "Sure, the farmers have them. They grow them and store them during winter in barns or cellars," he said.

That night, Herman had a dream. His mother and the girl from Piotrkow sat side by side on his bunk feeding him. He dreamt about food almost all the time now. Sometimes he saw a banquet maddeningly out of reach or like a mirage that evaporated as he came near. But on this night, as his dream visitors, his mother and the girl, fed him, Herman could taste the stew that they spooned into his mouth.

For the next month, Herman returned every day at the same time in hopes of seeing the girl by their section of the fence that was least patrolled. Many times she was there to toss him an apple. A couple of times she threw but missed. His mother had promised an angel to watch over him, but his angel was elusive. He couldn't get close enough to really see her, too dangerous. She loitered in the tree line and ran away after she had hit her target with the apples she threw. Then Herman would walk away with his heart beating hard, well aware that his game of Russian roulette couldn't continue for long. It was only a matter of time before a guard saw him and shot him. As it was, he was about to be punished for something entirely different.

A very bad cold snap came and had the prisoners shivering more than usual in their thin uniforms. One night, out in the wood, a kapo made a small fire. He stomped on old boxes and used the pieces to feed the modest pyre. The flames drew the men, almost as flimsy as moths, to gather round the glow and warm their hands. The fire was a unexpected treat that delighted Herman.

The next night, the kapo built another small blaze on the charred embers from the night before. Herman watched the flames lick at the wood and blessed the warmth it threw off. The fire was almost out when the air-raid sirens sounded. Herman knew the drill: the SS would run for cover to the bunkers and leave the prisoners to take their chances. Herman was happy. While the Allies dropped their bombs on distant Germans, he could stay outside with the other men and warm himself by the fire. He stooped, picked up a piece of broken crate, and jammed it into the dying fire where he saw an orange ember still glowed.

The sudden pain in Herman's head was excruciating. The hunch-backed SS Master was small but he had felled him with a single blow of his stick. As he lay on the ground, the Master beat the length of Herman's body, like a percussionist hitting an instrument. Then he returned to his head and face, striking at them with the metal base of his stick now. The blood was pouring from Herman's head, running down his face and into his eyes. The pain from his cracked skull was unimaginable. In his agony, he knew that somewhere in the group of men watching that at least one of his brothers stood powerless to help. Herman had seen the

Master beat men to death and he knew that he was about to suffer the same fate. He's going to kill me. Dear God, he is going to kill me.

Herman lay curled up on the ground, the blows striking his fingers that he pressed against his skull as useless protection. Pain from the blows hopscotched throughout his entire body, but it was the agony in his head that was bringing him to the edge of unconsciousness. The wail of the siren persisted—an ugly siren song. It called the beast that was savaging him back to the moment and his own imminent danger.

The SS Master suddenly stopped mid blow, straightened up and headed for the bunker. It was Sam who rushed to help his brother. "Get up, Herman. Get up," he said. But Herman couldn't get up. The pain and nausea, the faintness made it impossible to move. Herman felt his brothers half lead, half drag him into the cover of trees. They cleaned away the blood from his face and eyes. He opened them, but he still could not see.

The next day in his bunk, Herman slept when he could and prayed to fall into darkness, away from the unceasing pain in his head and the realization that he was blind. Each time he came to and opened his black swollen eyes, he still saw nothing. When the SS find out, they will shoot me, he thought. I want my mother. But today she didn't come and sit on his bunk. He heard his brothers gather around him. "Come on, Herman, get up. We have to go to work," Sam said. "I'm blind," Herman whimpered, hardly believing it.

"Not for long. Your sight will come back when the swelling goes down," Isydor said. He and Sam helped Herman to his feet, sandwiched him between them, and guided him to Appell, where they managed to hide the catastrophe from the SS. Then his brothers walked him through the woods towards the gieserei. Herman listened to the usual sounds: the screaming SS, the shuffle of weary prisoners. They sounded strange without the pictures to go with them. I'm done for, he thought. Any minute now an SS is going to see that I am blind and shoot me on the spot. Worse for my brothers than me. I don't want them to witness it.

"Herman, I am going to hide you in these trees," Sam said. "Don't move. Don't try to come out. I will come for you after the shift. DON'T MOVE." Herman felt the unexpected scratch and scrape of a branch pulling across his face and batted it away. Sam pushed his shoulders down and Herman bent his knees, slid his back down the tree trunk that was now bracing him, and rested his seat on a cold dry patch of ground. He heard the rustle as his brother took off and left him stranded against the tree.

He felt abandoned and his head was throbbing. He dozed and lost track of time. Anxiety began to ripple through him. I can't stay here. I have to get back. Reason was failing him. In the stillness of the dark wood, enshrouded in is blindness, Herman was taken over by the urge to run, to feel his way through the trees until he found his brothers. He began to walk. No better go back to the first spot where Sam left me, so he can find me. Where am I? Panic. No sense of direction or distance. Herman reached out for a tree trunk, found one, and wrapped his arms around it. Time went by. I'm lost. They won't find me. The dogs will come.

Throughout the long, slow creep of hours, Herman stood then sat, then stood again, his mind flip-flopping between panic and calm. He heard footsteps. Loud whispers: "Herman? Herman?" He turned and shuffled in the direction of the voice. "I'm here," he called.

"I told you not to move." Sam grabbed his hand and pulled him forward, out of the wood. Again, his brothers hustled him through the ordeal of Appell and then back to the barracks for bed. Herman balanced on the edge of sleep and conjured up people and places in his mind's eye. He thought about the girl at the fence near the edge of the wood. I won't see her again. I won't see anything again.

For two more days, his brothers sheltered him in the trees while they worked their shift. They hid his blindness from the SS during Appell, until Herman began to see again. At first only rippling light and shifting shadows played before his eyes. Then, on the fourth day, a blurred and shaky vision was restored.

Isydor was right, the SS were planning another transport. It was early April 1945. They had heard that the German offensive was in tatters and the Nazis were retreating. What to do about the Jews? Herman heard his brothers debating SS options. Why not just abandon the concentration and slave labor camps? Was it a neurotic compulsion to finish the job? To free Europe of the scourge of Jews? Or a massive clean-up operation? Dead men tell no lies and they cannot bear witness to criminal tribunals about what the SS had done; the same SS who would claim later that they were just following orders. Herman knew better. Like every other prisoner, he knew how much most SS relished cruelty; had a very keen personal appetite for torture. Time and time again, he had seen how they reveled in the suffering and degradation they doled out.

Herman and his brothers joined the column of men marching to the railroad siding. These aren't cattle cars, he thought. They were coal hoppers, filthy inside and open to the elements. It was April, but a feather-light snow was falling again. Where are we going? Herman didn't bother asking. Who knew? Those who did wouldn't tell. In the game of hide the Jew, what miserable corner remained as a hiding place? Nobody was saying. SS might be just days away from endgame and war lost, but they still had the power to say which Jew lived or died. Could still refuse to tell their busted-up captives where they were shunting them to next.

Yellow men, musulmen, skeletons, babbling crazy men and a few who looked like they still had some fight in them, Herman looked around at his fellow passengers in the open coal car. His brothers were there too, thank God. It's a miracle that we're all still together along with the honorary Rosenblat--Hesiek. How is it possible? How has Isydor kept his word all this time: where one goes we all go. Herman began to think about how breaking up their unit should seem like fruit ripe for the picking to an SS. We've managed to stay together since 1939. From Bydgoszcz to Wolborz to Piotrkow to Bugaj to Buchenwald to Schlieben. And now where? One of these days an SS will cotton and blow us all out, but maybe not today. He found a place in the squalor of the transport. What was worse, the stench of closed cattle cars, or the misery of riding open air in the snow?

This ride was turning out to be like the others: the hoppers were parked on sidings for the greater part of the day and in motion mostly at night. One night, Herman woke up freezing and under a crushing pressure. "GET OFF ME!" he cried then straightened up trying to shake off the weight on top of him. "Hey, get off!" He elbowed the man who did not move. Shit, he was dead! He wrestled the corpse upright and leaned it against the side of the car. The dead man's eyes and mouth were open in the ugliest twisted death mask. Herman felt nothing. No fear. No pity. Just annoyance because the dead man had disturbed his sleep. He yanked the guy's shirt, but the thin fabric tore. He pulled on the rag again and tried to cover the face and its awful expression. Then Herman leaned against the body like it was a makeshift pillow, but it was stiff already.

Herman closed his eyes, shifted about and tried to sleep. Unexpectedly, thoughts of Tatus came upon him; his father's corpse was the first dead body he had ever seen, so long ago. He remembered how they had lowered the body into the grave without a coffin. It had seemed so barbaric at the time, but he realized now that his father's burial was a luxury compared with what he had seen in the three years since: bodies tossed like garbage from trains or thrown in mass graves. Stacked like cords of wood, top to tail, in the morgue in Buchenwald; cadavers so emaciated that oftentimes, he knew, they were jammed, two at a time, into the crematorium's oven.

Herman pictured his beloved father, wrapped in his white prayer shawl, his kippah on his head. Weeping mourners had said Kaddish for him and his family had sat Shiva. Was his father one of the last Jews to receive these dignities before the Nazis yanked them all away and made death for Jews as depraved as they had made life? Herman remembered his father's dying words: "Don't hate anybody and always be tolerant. If you get out of this war alive, try not to bear a grudge."

"Tatus," Herman whispered to his father's ghost as he rode the coal hopper deeper into a new hell, "you had no idea what was in store for us when you said those words to me on your deathbed. You said don't bear a grudge, but what about the Nazis? Isn't it my duty to hate them? Doesn't God himself hate them for what they have done?" But Herman doubted that his father could hate anyone, not even the SS. Even if he could have seen what his youngest child had witnessed. "It would just break your heart, Tatus," Herman said, and then he heard the echo of his father's familiar response: "It can only be bad for a while and then it will get better again."

"How can it be, Tatus," Herman said, "that I am only 15 and already I know more about this world than you did when you left it?"

Herman looked at his dead companion, at his twisted face covered with a torn shirt. How long before I am lying dead like you, pushed in some corner in a pool of piss? Will anyone say Kaddish for me? Will there by any family left to care that I am dead and mourn for me? Herman felt ashamed. The train rumbled down the track and his cold, desperate comrades shivered and moaned as they tried to sleep on the hard floor of the stinking coal hopper.

Herman wanted to honor his dead father and the goodness he had taught all his sons. With a heart as full of love as he could make it, without the benefit of a congregation, and with his faltering Hebrew, Herman quietly repeated a line from the Mourner's Kaddish: "May there be abundant peace from heaven, and life, for us and for all Israel, Amen." He said the one line over and over again for his father, for the deceased and deserted neighbor beside him, and for all the Jews he did not know who were scattered across acres of torment. And then he went to sleep.

Two days without food and water or a stop to clean out the cars and the body count was rising. In Herman's car, crafty riders were wise in the ways of survival. They stacked the bodies into a neat pile to clear more room and create makeshift seating. But there was still the matter of the stench. The odor of death and human waste in the bottom of the car was unimaginable. Thank God, the hopper was open to the air. It wasn't so cold now. They were riding into warmer weather but Herman felt lethargic and more unwell that usual. His brow was hot and his face flushed. He was feverish. And his feet and legs were red and swollen, tight and tender to the touch. He wondered if it wasn't the beginning of the end for him. Sam was huddled beside him, hugging his legs, his chin resting on his knees. His square jaw still looked strong and even more angular in his shrunken face. Sam was a watcher, always scanning his environment, on the look out for fresh opportunity or danger. "Samek," Herman said and heard how hoarse his voice sounded.

"What?" Sam didn't look at him but kept up his hopper surveillance.

"Do you believe in God?" Herman asked.

"I suppose so," Sam said quietly.

"Why?"

"Because Tatus and Mamusia taught us to believe. That's what they would want us to do." He sounded flat and uninterested.

"Do you think they would still believe in God if they were here?"

"I don't know, probably."

"So you think they would still want us to believe in God no matter what?"

"Herman." Sam finally looked at him. "Shut up with the questions."

After a couple more days of stop and start, the train stopped again. It felt like for good this time. Destination reached. We're headed for a gas chamber for sure, Herman thought, but look at them, all they want to do is get off this train. The other prisoners were stirring from their zombie state, trying to pull themselves up to look over the edges of the car. Desperate now to be freed from the prison of the hopper. But they were doomed to languish for three more days in the siding. The rumors did the rounds. The camp or wherever it was they were headed did not want to accept the shipment of men. Herman looked around at the filthy forest of rags and bones in the car with him. Who could blame them? Maybe the SS were finally sick of cleaning up and disposing of all this human wreckage they had created.

Herman was feverish and sleeping a lot. "Come on Herman,

get up and try to walk," Isydor said, pulling on him as he dozed, crumpled and sweating in the bottom of the hopper. "It's time to leave." But Herman could not move. The most unbelievable stupor had come over him. He looked up at Isydor with exhausted eyes, black valleys underneath them. I just can't go on. He couldn't even say the words. He heard SS screaming at them to get out and move on: Raus! Raus! What a blessing if an SS shot me and put me out of my misery, he thought. I can't walk through another set of. I can't face what is coming next. But his brothers were stubborn. They hoisted him up and carted him along towards their new abode: the show camp. The jewel in the crown of SS concentration camps. The Rosenblats had arrived in Czechoslovakia at Theresienstadt, the camp that Hitler gave to the Jews.

Chapter Twelve
Liberation

It was a camp, Herman saw, but it was also a town. The whole town was a great walled ghetto. This was Theresienstadt. It had begun as an eighteenth century fortress and later became a prison. In 1940, the SS had converted it into a concentration camp and a stopping-off point for Jews as they passed through on their way to Auschwitz mostly. Herman did not know that he was entering famous territory.

Just the previous June, the Danish Red Cross had requested a visit to check on the conditions of Danish Jews being held in the camp. The SS had spruced the place up: planted flowers, set up fake shops with food in the windows, and even arranged for a children's choir to perform an original composition. A Jewish theater director was ordered to make a movie about the amenities of Camp Theresienstadt that demonstrated Hitler's largesse in giving the Jews a city of their own. A place where the Jewish people, their musicians, intellectuals, and cultural elite could live in beneficial conditions. The Red Cross came, they saw, they left; they were satisfied with what they found in Theresienstadt. The

Jews who had cleaned up the camp, acted in the propaganda film, and helped direct the charade, were sent to Auschwitz.

Now in April 1945, to the annoyance of the Camp Commandant, thousands more Jews were being herded through Theresienstadt, joining the never-ending queue for their turn in the gas chambers that were running around-the-clock at Auschwitz.

Herman limped off the train at the Bohusovice railway station and through the gates of Camp Theresienstadt. He passed prisoners loitering in the narrow stone streets. Every one of them seemed reduced to the same desperate appearance. An army of hunched, emaciated cadavers in grimy striped uniforms with shaved heads, boney faces, yellow skin and ears sticking out. They cheered as Herman and the men in his transport, who looked the same as they did, marched by. Yes, Herman realized, the inmates really are cheering our little rag-tag band of half-dead Jews, just off the train from Schlieben. Cheering us like we are a liberating army. Or maybe they were cheering because every Jew who staggered in, still standing, after six long years, was nothing short of a miracle.

Herman's column marched across the bridge into the Little Fortress, through an archway crowned with a sign made of great metal letters: Arbecht Macht Frei. Work makes you free. Ah yes, but Herman was too exhausted for irony. They passed through a courtyard with stone buildings on three sides. But despite the sprawl of courtyards and building around them and beyond, the guards crammed prisoners into only a small corner of the complex. All the better to guard them, Herman supposed.

Herman was one of 12 men pushed into a single room. He crashed onto a bed, his swollen legs throbbing. Thank God, they were allowed to lie down because there was no way he could stand and move around. This was not a work camp, he could tell. And even if it were, judging by the look of the Jews brought here, nothing would get done. Every ounce of work had been wrung out of the human dregs that now made it to Theresienstadt. It was time, no doubt, for the SS to put them all down. Herman was absolutely positive that the specter of the gas chamber that had been haunting him since Piotrkow had finally caught up with him. Who cares? he thought. I'll just lie here and sleep until they come for me. But Isydor wouldn't let him sleep.

"Herman, get up and walk." Over the next few days, Isydor was insistent; no playing games. "There will be a serious infection, if you don't keep moving and help the swelling go down," his brother argued. Who cares? Herman thought again, but he was so used to doing what Isydor said. He leaned on his brothers and endured the agony of limping as best he could for 20 minutes at a time outside the room and down the halls and sometimes even into the courtyard.

Locked behind impenetrable gates, the prisoners were free to roam the complex. There was no way to escape. And who had the energy? Lethargic prisoners lay around, weak and starving. Many looked too ill to grasp who or where they were.

"Damn the lice." Herman worked his swollen legs and muttered. The pain was everywhere. From the SS who loved the taste of beating prisoners with sticks, to the disease that ravaged their shrunken bodies, and the lice that fed on them constantly. Every millimeter of a Jew was marked for misery.

Germans tossed them the odd ration but the usual obsessive order of camp life was missing. No work. No roll-call. It was like they were abandoned here in a strange limbo. Waiting. For what? Herman remembered that his life used to be divided into days and nights, weeks and months. But the SS had gifted him with the endless day. Days ran into one another and no one marked time. No one ever knew what day, or month, or even year it was. Now they waited, cooped up in this labyrinth of stone chambers and courtyards of Theresienstadt as more days ran into one another. Everyone knew that this was the last stop. The men here were diseased and starved and they were dying in hoards. The bodies were stacked in rooms and in the courtyard and as the weather grew warm, the awful stench permeated the air. The whole camp smelled like it was in decay as Herman inhaled the sweet, sickly molecules of death.

Prisoners kept watch and announced whenever more Jews arrived. Now they were part of the cheering section too. Like the crowd that waits on the finishing line at the end of a very long race, they were rooting for the Jews who had somehow hung on and were stumbling into Theresienstadt. But what would the brave souls get for making it so far? Death like everyone else, probably. Herman started to think that the ones he had seen die first, back in 1942, were the lucky ones. Just keep going. Get through one more day. He and his brothers had whispered this injunction each and every day to keep each other alive. For what?

Herman was disgusted but he was starting to feel better. The swelling in his legs was subsiding. They were almost their normal size and he didn't feel quite so exhausted. One day, he was lying in the communal cell, when he heard a loud rumbling. Sam darted out and returned just minutes later. He skidded into the doorway. "A tank. A tank," he shouted and took off again. "Russians," a prisoner yelled from another cell. "The Russians are here!" For a few minutes, Herman sat listening to the crack of gunfire, a few volleys back and forth. Shouting in the courtyard and beyond. And then came the most unbelievable announcement from down the hall: We are free!

"The camp has been under the supervision of the Red Cross for over a week," Isydor said when he came back from his fact-finding mission. "And a Russian platoon, diverted from Prague, was sent to liberate us. Most of the Germans have gone. The Russians have taken the few hold-outs prisoner." Herman listened to his brother's report. That's it? No bombing raid? No heavy fighting? Just a half-hearted skirmish? The Russians rolled through the gates of Theresienstadt and the few Germans who were left turned on their heels, fired a few rounds, or put up a white flag.

Herman stood in the courtyard and watched Russians buzz around the camp, reveling in their role as liberators, smiling, waving and handing out food--beans mostly. Herman was ravenous, hovering over Isydor as he opened their haul of supplies. But his big brother put the breaks on overeating. Herman watched as the food miser spooned just a taste of the new rations they were drooling over into their metal cups and then put the rest away. "Please Isydor, I'm starving. Give me more," Herman begged.

"Your body can't digest protein and fat," Isydor said. "It will kill you." Herman glowered, watching other prisoners stuff themselves with the food they had been deprived for so long.

But Isydor was right. On his bunk that night, Herman lay awake listening to the moans, to the sickening sounds of retching and diarrhea. Overeating by starving men was taking its toll. The food they craved was killing them. There was an epidemic of dysentery, as well as the ever-present typhus, and then a new and dangerous outbreak of diphtheria. Liberated prisoners were free to roam the camp, but they were still imprisoned with the gates closed and the camp placed under quarantine. The Russians had locked up their German captives. They were released now on camp clean-up duty and no one seemed too worried that they might get sick.

Herman whiled away the long hours ambling around the camp. It felt good to just stand outdoors in the courtyard warmed by the sunshine and free from the incessant barking of SS orders. One day, he passed a German solider who was cleaning a stinking latrine used by Jews now under the care of the Red Cross. Prisoners were so ill that they were shitting out their insides. Here was the solider retching, his head turned to the side, away from the stench, as he worked with the filthy mop to clean up the vile watery waste.

Herman remembered the cattle cars. Scooping waste with his hands and tossing it outside next to the corpses of dead riders. He felt a strange, potent, and unpleasant mixture of feelings as he stood and watched the German: hatred and contempt and delight at seeing his enemy humiliated by the disgusting task. You can never suffer like we have, he thought. How can we ever make you suffer like we have? I would like to try, but what could I possibly do? How can you ever know a fraction of the pain you have inflicted?

Herman walked away and felt suddenly depressed and empty. Revenge felt bad; didn't offer the satisfaction he thought it would. In Schlieben, he used to lie on his bunk plotting--contemplating the punishment he would devise to pay back the SS for the torment they caused. Now, it was unsettling to realize he didn't have what it took to pursue pay-back. Revenge was an empty, depressing feeling. Just another lousy emotion courtesy of the Nazis: hunger, misery, illness, grief and revenge. All bad. All futile.

With the camp under quarantine, the streets beyond the camp gates were off-limits, but Herman and Sam snuck out with other wily prisoners to roam and scrounge for supplies. Sam had always been a top-notch scavenger. Now, he thrived on sneaking in and out on foraging missions. He came back from his excursions with exotic foods like meats and cheeses. And with clothes: the incomparable haul of boots and jackets. One afternoon, Herman watched as Sam came back to their room with a big brown sack and an ear-to-ear grin. He emptied a mound of booty on the floor and then stood back with his arms folded as his brothers and cousins mixed and matched clothing until they were all kitted out in the right sizes more or less.

Now, they were all bathed, in clean clothes, and fed. And they had shoes! And socks! Herman had been convinced that he would never own shoes again. In Schlieben, he had traded his old bust-up shoes for bread and another prisoner's worn-out pair. You couldn't even really call them shoes. They were just two soles with no uppers. Herman had tied them to his feet with rags.

Now, he looked down at his new shoes, turning his feet this way and that. What a marvelous thing! Well, they weren't exactly new, but they weren't falling apart. He felt strangely happy. Stupid! They were only shoes. He was feeling better all way round, just back from the infirmary and the kind doctor who had examined him. He was a member of the special delegation that was here to care for the children. The doctor had listened to Herman's heart with a stethoscope, smiling up at him. Your heart is beating strong and I'm glad, his wink said. Next, he looked in Herman's eyes with a light and gently fingered the boy's scars from measles and beatings and infected bites.

Herman was proud. Isydor had done it again. A Czech officer was now Commandant of Theresienstadt. Despite all the prisoners in his care and the matters competing for his attention, Isydor's intelligence and unmatched talent for organization had stood out to the new boss man. He tapped Isydor to help out at the children's camp with all its sick and displaced youngsters. Make sure that short-term they are fed and clothed and brought back to health, he instructed. And long-term that they are reunited with family, if possible, or placed with organizations that can start rehabilitating them.

Sam was always on the prowl looking for food, clothes and supplies, but Abraham caught something else: a pretty Polish girl he met in the camp. She was a pharmacist and she spoke perfect French. She was applying for papers to live in France. Abraham wanted to go with her. "I can look for Eva while I am there," Abraham said when he sat on his bed and announced his plans to his brothers. No one knew if Eva was still alive even.

Herman felt rattled. War and life in the camps had dictated that they always stick together and were never apart for more than a few minutes. Their lives had depended on it. Now peace was going to break them up? Lutek said he wanted to take his chances with Abraham in France. Barak wanted desperately to get to Palestine. He was heading out for a displaced persons camp in Germany. He'd heard that he could get papers and transport from there.

"Where are we going?" Herman asked Isydor one day.

"The Commandant has asked me to work with a Jewish organization from England," Isydor said. "It is called the Committee for the Care of Children from Concentration Camps. Isaac Finkelstein and I are arranging to take more than 300 kids from Theresienstadt to England, so that we can get to work finding them homes while the organization looks for their families."

"Am I going?" Herman asked.

"Yes, Sam is going to help me and you will come with us."

"And Hesiek." Herman named the honorary Rosenblat.

"And Hesiek too." Isydor assured him.

In all the years he had been in the camps, struggling just to make it through one more day day, Herman had not really contemplated the realities of what would happen after the war. Where they would go. Where they would live. I suppose three out of five isn't so bad, he thought now. Isydor, Sam and I in England. Abraham and Eva, pray God she's still alive, in France. France and England, but no more Poland—their homeland. No more Tatus and Mamusia. This was the day he had both hoped for and dreaded. The day that marked the start of the new life he would begin if the war ever came to and end. If any of them were still left standing. But it was also a day of reckoning. For adding up the losses and realizing that his life, derailed by the Nazis for six years, was about to resume on an unfamiliar and unexpected course. Nothing or next to nothing of his old life remained. It would all begin over from scratch.

"Cocoa, children. Come in here and have some cocoa." The lady in the cheerful flowered dress was doing a stiff-handed clap and directing the children to take a cup of cocoa from the table in the reception hall where they were gathered. "Everyone, please do get some cocoa."

English. It was a strange language and Herman wanted to learn it, but not now; he was too tired. He had had a taste of the new tongue on the plane--the big Lancaster bomber. He had sat cross-legged, singing songs in Yiddish and Hebrew with the other kids on the floor of the giant plane that had no windows. It was like being in the belly of some great beast with engines that roared. But the kids were happy and excited. Ten planes had been commissioned to transport the more than 300 young Jewish refugees from Prague to an airbase in the north of England. As they droned through the skies on the short flight, Herman practiced a few English words to pass the time away. The important ones: May I have something to eat, please. Excuse me but do you have some chocolate? Apparently, they did. The children were now helping themselves to hot chocolate in white pot mugs. But Herman was too exhausted to understand the kind, efficient lady who welcomed him with a hot beverage.

When the giant Lancaster Bombers had deposited their cargo--the party of boys and its handful of girls, at the air force base, the kids had climbed onto waiting buses. They were headed for Windermere in the bucolic Lake District. But Herman's bus had broken down and lost a couple of hours waiting for repairs. When it took off again, night was falling, as they wound through narrow roads flanked by stone walls. Beyond these uneven, ancient walls, Herman saw a patchwork of fields of the most spirit-raising green, populated with flocks of docile sheep, heads down munching on grass.

Herman was affected by the vibrant colors. In the camps, color had been leeched from everything. Washed away by grief itself: the black of smoke and SS uniforms, gray barren barracks buildings and bunks, the frigid white of winter and parched yellow skins of decaying prisoners. Not a blade of grass. Not a touch of home. No hue of kindness anywhere.

It was dark when they finally reached their destination—a children's camp. Camp? What an unfortunate choice of word. And most of the young travelers were asleep, slumped against each other or against the windows, and drooling on the glass. Herman stood with his exhausted travel pals in their new home; too beat to wonder what might happen next.

He drank down the warm cocoa. Nice. Draining the dark mixture of powdery dregs from the bottom of the cup. Never refuse food or waste anything. Then he followed the lady who could not speak German or Polish and who made up for it by smiling constantly. She led Herman and Hesiek up a staircase, down a long hallway, and into a small cheery bedroom that had two beds made up with the crispest, cleanest, whitest cotton sheets. Herman climbed into the fresh single bed and had just enough time, before passing out, to realize that he was, in fact, in heaven.

Next morning, the woman interviewing Herman looked neat and trim in a white blouse and grey skirt. Women, along with color, were making a welcome return to his world. He tried to examine this new lady without her noticing. She was not very young, but she looked pretty and smelled good like flowers. He kept leaning in to catch another whiff. Herman liked the way her brown hair was tucked under at her neck and pulled up on both sides of her head into wings--little wings of hair. These new caregivers did seem a bit like angels. "I will send an angel to watch over you," Mamusia had promised. The lady wore little round pearl earrings.

Women were certainly interesting. This one was called Mrs. Morrison. She was originally from Poland, but she had lived in England for a very long time. She was Jewish and spoke Polish. She was explaining that during his stay, Herman would be learning to speak English and to read and write it. He would be eating and sleeping and spending a lot of time outdoors. Swimming and riding bicycles and hiking and relaxing. Getting his strength back.

"I know you have family here," Mrs. Morrison said, hesitating over the word family.

"Yes I have my two brothers and Hesiek," Herman said.

"But not your parents?" Now she hesitated over the word parents. This was a first for Herman. The first time to tell someone what had happened to his parents. What was the best way to go about it? How to form the briefest explanation? There had been no tea parties and mixers in the concentration camps. Everyone knew why they there: to die. No one asked about missing parents. Everyone knew the answer already: dead probably.

"My father died of typhus in Wolborz ghetto," Herman said. "My mother was sent to Treblinka to be gassed." The woman leaned back a little and jerked her head as though she had looked under the lid of a box to find an ugly surprise. Should Herman say something to make her feel better about the fact that his parents had died in such an ugly manner?

"Well, we don't need to think about those things now, my dear," the woman said putting the lid back on the box and straightening herself up. Ah, Herman realized without even thinking about it. I get it. I understand the rule. Outside the camp, we don't talk about inside the camp. Fine by me. From then on, whenever anyone asked Herman about his parents, and tried to look under the lid, he knew to keep it tight shut. No peeking. "My parents died in the war," he would say, with the most marvelous grasp of British understatement.

This children's camp was a first for Herman too. It was designed to bring people back to life and not hurry them towards death. The Lake District, Herman learned, despite his complete lack of interest, had been a muse to the great 19th century poet, Shelley. The diehard romantic had wandered its fields, drawing inspiration from its views. It was a moist, verdant, breezy paradise of crystal lakes and rolling hills and tended fields, quaint and charming, and set in its ways.

Herman and the kids from the camp set out to explore the countryside, to conquer it, and let it breathe new life into them too. They hiked across fields and swam in lakes and rode on sit-up-and-beg bikes. They rang their little tringing bike bells to tell pedestrians and farmers in their flat caps, who were out walking in the narrow lanes, to please move out the way. A bunch of kids thrilled to be alive and outdoors in the fresh air and on their way back to get tea at the camp—the good camp not the bad one--were coming through. If you don't mind.

Herman and the gang of rescued kids took it all in and slowly began to thrive despite the tuberculosis that a few had smuggled in on their lungs. They learned to speak faltering English. They came out of their shells, arguing and fighting. They stole food or extra servings and hid them under sweaters at almost every mealtime. Just in case mealtime should suddenly stop. They got angry when the new clothes they had been promised did not arrive on time. They had been denied for so long, it was intolerable now that anyone should refuse or withhold or delay any item that had been offered. It was like a collective exhalation. They had survived hadn't they? Barely. So for God's sake now, let the business of living move full-speed ahead, no delays or interruptions.

Just as he had lived life one day at a time in the old camp, so now did Herman live one day at a time in the new camp. He soaked up each and every day not thinking or planning ahead. But one day, after a number of weeks, Isydor came and sat on his bed.

"Sam and I are going to London," Isydor said without preamble. Life in the camps had always dictated that communication between them be shorthand and direct.

"I'm coming too," Herman said.

"No." Isydor did not hesitate. "You are staying here. You have the chance to study and learn English. Some people in London have offered to help Sam and me find a place to live and work. You have a big opportunity to benefit from what the CCCC is offering you. So please, Herman, have the sense not to fight me and understand that I ask this because it is good for you."

Herman put up a fuss, but it was minimal. He was nearly 16. Not a child in danger who needed protection from older bothers, but a young adult who should be able to recognize his best bet when he saw it. He still had Hesiek. That night, he watched his friend sleeping and felt his mother's safeguarding presence. "Thank you for watching over me, Mamusia," he whispered like a prayer. He believed that she always had and always would bring the people and things to him that he needed to survive.

Then, Herman lay awake in the dark of a moonless night and tried not to see the inky blackness as a projection screen that his mind could use to play its reels of cruel recordings. In Piotrkow, he remembered, Isydor had promised that after the war they would all start a new life, a good one. Herman decided to trust his brother's prediction. After all, he had been a pretty good oracle up until now.

Chapter Thirteen
Roma

It was a long way to drive from the Bronx down the whole length of Manhattan and out to Coney Island, but his friend, Dave, said that the girl was worth it. She worked as a nurse with his girlfriend, Sadie, and she was a real looker. And had he mentioned that she was Polish? It would be a great double date.

"What's her name?" Herman asked. Dave screwed up his face and inhaled loudly through pursed lips. "I can't remember," he said. "I never met her."

"Then how do you know she's a looker?" Herman had a bad feeling.

"Because Sadie told me." Dave diverted his eyes from the road to look at the blind-date victim, who was squirming in the passenger seat, and he grinned.

Herman hated dating in general and blind dates in particular. The mindless chit chat, trying to find common interests. The way the girls were often stiff and skittish, because they thought you might try to come on too strong. The girls who were pretty but still not your type. The girls who were your type, but not interested, or interested, but still the chemistry was wrong. Oy! At least at Coney Island, there would be plenty of distractions. Still it was a long way to drive from the Bronx to Coney Island.

The hot city air rode the light breeze that came in through the car's open windows. Herman fell quiet as he thought about his love life. He had played the field. Now, he was ready to find the "one" and forget the ones that had got away. There had been the beautiful shiksa on the Queen Mary when he first immigrated to America back in 1950. When they saw he was all alone on the big ship, her parents had kindly invited him to join their party. They had been gracious hosts until they smelled romance between their teenage daughter and the young Jew without any means whom they had befriended. Then Herman was no longer welcome at their table, persona non grata, and the pretty daughter was chaperoned and placed off limits.

There was no barbed wire fence on the ship, Herman thought. No SS with a dog and a stick, just a subtle prejudice. No harm intended but I'm not comfortable with your kind dating my kind. Just an acorn of bigotry that given enough time and attention could be nurtured into the mighty oak of genocide. Herman had curled up in his bunk and wept. Yes wept. In disillusionment and frustration and anger.

After six weeks in New York, living with Sam and his wife, Herman was called up for service. Yes, the American Government was happy to welcome Herman Rosenblat to America. Now, here is a uniform and there is Korea. Except Herman was not deployed to combat. He looked heavenward when he got his assignment as an army electrician. "Thank you, Mamusia."

Next, he was sent to Trieste in Italy and there in the land of pretty women and great food, he was engaged. Twice. To two beautiful girls. They both inspired first marriage, and later, cold feet. Then came a short visit to Palestine and a beautiful, spunky nurse. She seemed so right for him but the timing was so wrong.

Now Herman was back in New York. He was 28 and the owner of Herman's Television, his own TV repair business. He was ready for what came next. He was ready for "the one". The real one that would move him regret-free from bachelorhood to wedded bliss. His brothers were all married and settled. Abraham had married his Polish chemist and settled in France. And he had made good on his promise to locate Eva. She had made it out to Palestine and then returned to France to reunite with her brother. Abraham sent the good news to Isydor who was living in London. In fact, he sent more than good news. He asked a lovely young Polish woman who was going on a visit to England to bring the message to his brother. He must have known the woman might be right for Isydor and his hunch was dead on, because Isydor courted and married the attractive bearer of good tidings.

Next, Sam had found his Miss Right in London where he was living and working and struggling to pick up English. His wedding was the event that enabled the longed-for day that Herman had dreamed about: all his brothers and Eva reunited in celebration. His throat was tight and he couldn't talk when he walked into Sam's apartment and found his sister sitting there on a chair by the window in a silver shaft of brilliant sunlight. After eight long years of separation, she was as beautiful, as kind, and as loving as he had always remembered her—his wonderful Eva.

Now only young Herman was left a bachelor. After his stint at the camp in Windermere, he had been assigned to complete an intensive training course in English at Ascot in the south of England for four months. After that, he was on his own, turned loose by the Jewish Committees that had invested in his rehabilitation. It was 1946 and he was ready to be a productive, upstanding citizen of the world. A world he believed was ready to treat him in his approaching manhood a little better than it had during his desperate boyhood. His trusty companion, Hesiek, was still with him and they decided to move up to London and room together to be near Isydor and Sam. Herman tried out at various jobs— leather cutting and as an electrician and TV repairman. Then Sam moved to America with his wife and settled. He found a sponsor for Herman, the one brother who still had no ties, and invited the youngest Rosenblat to sail to an exciting new world and make a fresh start. Now, it was seven years later—1957 and Herman was 28 and a traveled man of the world.

"And this is my friend, Roma." Sadie yanked Roma's arm and pulled her slightly off balance as she presented the beautiful young woman to Herman. Yes, of course he heard angels singing. They always sing at perfection. The beautiful dark curly hair cut short but oh so feminine. The lovely warm brown almond eyes. The curves of a petite figure and the soft fragrant skin of bare arms he could tell had been dabbed with perfume. The warmth she exuded. And a sense of play. Beauty? Check. Chemistry? Check. Love at first sight? Check. How wonderful that it was such a long ride from the Bronx to Coney Island and he could sit in the back seat with Roma and talk at high speed in Polish, because she was still stiff in English.

Doesn't food taste amazing when you are high on attraction? Aren't colors brighter and the racing moments somehow filled with more charge and possibility? At Coney Island, Herman had to put his arm around Roma's delicate shoulders in the gently swaying gondola of the Ferris wheel, because it was a little chill at the top where the wheel had made it's half turn and held them suspended in the air as they waited for the ride to fill. And he had to pull her closer, because the view of the water and the city above the lights and music and colors of the amusement park was so beautiful. It needed nearness to make it better.

A summer night, long and warm. Herman and Roma lounged on the beach, leaning back and bracing themselves on their bare arms, as they buried and wiggled their bare toes in the sand. They talked of the recent past and soon used it all up. It was time, if they chose, to go back further in their personal history, to the war. Always difficult. "My parents died in the war," Herman said and he saw that Roma understood the code. She put her pretty chin down a little and gazed off into the water. But it was a message to go on if he wanted, not to stop talking about his painful past. You don't have to put a lid on it, she was saying.

"My brothers and I were in the ghettos and the camps from 1939 to 1945," Herman continued. He listed the old names on his fingers: Wolborz, Piotrkow, Bugaj, Buchenwald, Schlieben and Theresienstadt like they were stops along the way on some tour through hell that he had somehow survived and efficiently cata-logued. No need to dramatize or paint the graphic picture. They both knew the score for Jews on the war front. It was hard and long and brutal. They had been terrified, starving and desperate.

"What about you? Where were you in the war?" Herman asked Roma after a while.

"My father was a metal worker in Poland near Lodz," she said and Herman remembered that there had been a big ghetto there in Lodz.

"Before they began deporting Jews to camps," Roma said, "my father was doing a lot of work for the Catholic church. He went to them and they agreed to give us birth certificates saying that we were Catholics. And then my father volunteered to go work on a farm in Germany. My parents and my sister and I went. We had to leave my baby sister with my aunt in Poland. She was supposed to bring her later but they couldn't get out in time and they died in the ghetto. She was only three." Roma looked at Herman and pressed her eyes shut for a while to mark the end of the tragic verse about her lost baby sister. "We lived and worked on the farm," she went on. "We passed as Christians and went to mass. We were always afraid that we would be found out."

Herman listened. He was impressed that Roma's father had been resourceful enough to hide his family in plain sight. And he was sympathetic. He knew about the disruption, the unraveling of family life. The worry they must have felt at the separation from the little one and the sadness and guilt when she did not survive. All survivors, he knew, had lived through a variation on the same theme: they were pitched into a violent sea, frightened and displaced, tossed around in the Nazi storm, never knowing if and when calm would ever return.

Roma could picture Herman as a boy: motherless, traumatized and starving. She was sorry that she could not have rescued him. She had not been unaware as a child of how other Jews were suffering. "When I was a girl passing as a Christian," she told him as they talked, "I saw a Jewish boy and I threw him an apple. I wanted to help him." She recalled the far-off incident; the sudden impulse that she knew now could have cost her life.

Herman lounged in the sand, side by side with Roma, reveling in the sudden rightness of their new twoness. The instant togetherness that their meeting had instigated. A heavenly fusion. "That boy was me," Herman said and he smiled at the beautiful angel by his side.

When they finally stood up to go find Dave and Sadie, Roma bent down and picked something up from the sand: a small snapshot of Herman, as a child, with his Mamusia. She studied it for a moment. "This is yours," she said as she handed the photograph to him.

Chapter Fourteen
Love Story

Herman pulled up in front of Rabbi Oberman's house. His counselor worked out of a small cement extension built onto the home's main residence. Herman checked his watch. He was 20 minutes early. It was too hot to wait in the car, so he got out, and ambled up the brick path, dressed in his Florida uniform of lightweight pants and short-sleeved shirt. He stooped a little now, but Herman was still quite tall and vigorous with a full head of dark hair, clear lively eyes, a smiling mouth and almost unnaturally smooth skin. No lines or wrinkles. It seemed impossible that anyone who had lived through the stress and horror that Herman had should emerge at almost 80 with skin so smooth and untouched by pain. He opened the door to the anteroom just outside the office where the Rabbi met with people. He sat down in the small waiting room, ignoring the spread of magazines on a side table. A few seconds later, Rabbi Oberman opened the door and popped his head out. "Ah, Herman it's you. You're early," he said.

"Yes, I can wait here and finish my coffee if that's okay." Herman held up the half-finished cup of Dunkin Donuts coffee.

"That's fine." The Rabbi smiled and closed the door.

Last week, when Herman was leaving their appointment, the Rabbi had asked him if he would come this week prepared to talk about the book controversy and the fall-out. "Herman, we've touched on it," the Rabbi said, "but if you don't mind talking about it, I'd like to hear more from you about how you think this whole situation happened?"

"Sure, I can tell you about it," Herman had agreed.

Herman had come early today to gather his thoughts and put them in order so that he could give the Rabbi the shorthand version of events. He sat now, sipping his Dunkin Donuts coffee, and thinking back to the weeks in 1992, right after he had been shot. He had come home from the hospital still thinking about the dream, it was more like an apparition: his mother sitting on his hospital bed, telling him to write his life story. "Tell you story so your grandchildren will know what happened to their grandfather," she had said.

Herman was determined to do it, to write a book, but how? The Nazis had robbed him of any schooling beyond the second-grade. He had had a little home tutoring from Abraham in Wolborz and there had been a few months in England when he had studied hard to learn to speak English and to read and write it a little, but no formal education. He had studied to be an electrician and, over the years, he had developed an appetite for certain books and newspapers and television documentaries, but that didn't mean he could write a book, in English yet. Still, he had decided, he was going to give it a try. He sat down at his computer at the house in Brooklyn and began to write his account of how he had survived the Holocaust.

It was at this point that Herman found himself faced with the essential challenge confronting all storytellers: when he was done giving his shoah or survivor account, finished recounting all the desperate episodes of his young life during the war and immediately after, what then did he want his message to be? What do I, Herman Rosenblat, a child of the Holocaust, one of the last in a dwindling group of survivors, want people to learn from my story?

He knew what was at stake. The carnage of World War II, the suffering and death of tens of millions of Jews and non-Jews, was one of the worst crises of human making. The tragedy was a huge scar on man's psyche. A story that had been told again and again by survivors who tried to speak their truth before time and the tide erased them and the horror of their singular experiences. So what could be learned from Herman? From the degraded experiences of an ignorant child who survived only by clinging to his brothers, to dreams of his dead mother, and his belief in the guardian angels she sent to watch over him?

Herman discovered that he had never really drawn any conclusions about the insanity of the war years. Maybe because I never allowed myself to think about them, he realized. Now, as he switched on the light of a failing memory and shone it around the dark storehouse of his mind, he found that it was difficult and painful to remember too many details and to recall any long unbroken sequence of days in those years from 1939-1945. He did know that it was a time when one terror morphed into another. When the sole monotonous aim of every day was to dig your nails into life and hold on, dangling over the precipice of extinction, dictated by the Nazis and their Aryan ideal of a master race that had the obligation to wipe out what they believed were other inferior specimens.

Herman's mind strained to bridge the gap and recall the war years. What leapt out first were the experiences that had lived on most vividly in his memory and affected him most deeply. What do you remember the most? Herman asked himself, as he sat down to write, and the answer came back: I remember love. Of course he was overwhelmed by the memory of how sordid and degrading his experiences had been. The despair during times when he was sure that he couldn't walk though one more hopeless day because they were all filled with the same suffering and brutality. But as he looked back now, he saw that in some ways all the despair was just a backdrop. Against it, he could clearly see the people who had loved him and it made their love shine more brightly.

Herman returned again and again to thoughts of his father whose heart had never hardened. On his deathbed, Tatus had told him not to bear a grudge and to tolerate everyone. "I tried to take your advice," Herman whispered to his dead father. "And I've lived all the better for it." He knew that in a way Tatus' example had inoculated all his sons against bitterness. "You stopped us from getting angry about the things we couldn't change, Tatus. It's pointless to get angry. It just erodes your peace of mind and stops you from getting on with life."

Herman thought of his mother. You gave me life twice: once when I was born and a second time in Piotrkow, when you chased me away you and death in Treblinka. You forced me to stay with my brothers where I had a chance to survive. Even in death, you watched over me, Mamusia.

Memories of his brothers and sister came. Eva, you always loved and nurtured me. You paid off the bullies in Bydgoszcz. Isydor, Abraham and Samuel. Where one goes, we all go. You shared your rations, even though you were starving, because you believed I was growing and needed your food more than you did. You lifted me towards fresh air and light in the death trains. You always kept me close, sandwiched between you in the stinking bunks of Buchenwald. And you watched out for me when we worked, side by side, in the Bugaj lumberyard and at the slave camps.

Herman knew that the Nazis had been systematic in destroying their victims: alienate them from society, destroy their customs and liberties, concentrate them in camps, isolate them from meaningful contact, then starve, beat or murder what was left. But the Nazis never succeeded in destroying the bond between my brothers and me, Herman thought. We had solidarity. We nurtured each other and held onto hope during six dark years. If one or more of us had been dragged to our deaths, then maybe we would all have perished, but because we were a team, a working, self-protecting, self-sustaining unit, we survived.

Herman spent days at a time thinking about his account. Not just what had happened, but what it meant. In all their years of marriage, he and Roma had not dwelled too much on what they had both gone through during the war years: he trying to outrun the Nazi death machine and Roma trying to pass as a Christian, living in plain sight of danger at all times. For the first time, Herman began to dig deep and talk to Roma about those cruel years. She sat and listened quietly, like always. She had always created a happy home with a quiet presence. Years ago, Roma had told him about the incident that she would later repeat: "When I was a child passing as a Christian," she said, "I saw a Jewish boy and I threw him an apple. I wanted to help him."

"That boy was me," Herman had said that first night they met and he believed that somehow Roma had caught his meaning. He was saying that he believed her love could save him. That it could stretch into the past and save the boy he had been. Stretch into the future and save the man he would become. And he had been right. There was not a day that went by in their more than 50 years of marriage that Herman was not happy to have Roma Rosenblat.

Herman decided he would call his book, "The Will to Survive".

That's what they had been blessed with, the few who survived the camps. He began to write. He tapped out the pages and they poured out of him, rough and clumsy, but flowing freely. He tried to tell it all: the painful events, the childhood imaginings. Those times, when almost in a trance, his mind separated itself from his tortured body and simply went elsewhere. Herman explored his thoughts, his feelings, his adult conclusions, childish beliefs; the insights he had received during the grotesque chapters of his boyhood.

He re-conjured the dreams that had occurred over and over after the trauma of losing his mother. She was processed and herded, like an animal in an abattoir. Sent into a gas chamber to die, stripped of hope and dignity, in a way that he still could not and never would be able to think about. He preferred to remember how she had lived on in his dreams, watching over him and promising him an angel to love him. There was no question that Roma was the angel his mother had promised. Roma supported me through the lean early years of our marriage, Herman remembered, when I was uneducated, barely trained, and struggling to build a future for us.

Back then, Herman was still working as a TV repairman and Roma stayed home with their two small children. He would come home to their Brooklyn apartment in time for Roma to leave for work as a nurse on the nightshift. This ships-passing-in-the-night routine went on for years as they scraped together a living and a home. Roma never complained, always pulled alongside him. But then, what was to complain about? They had both witnessed the alternatives. They knew what could have been. They were grateful for every second of life they were given. Life was all. Hardship didn't matter.

Herman knew that he was destined to meet Roma. Years

before their first meeting, he had felt the promise of her as he came of age in the unnatural hellhole of a Nazi concentration camp. He had passed from a boy to a young man in this awful place, made the critical transitions to manhood--physical, spiritual and psychological. Despite his undernourished body and spirit, he had managed to dream and fantasize about physical and emotional love with a woman. Herman wanted to believe that Roma had been there with him all along. After she first told him her story, he began to imagine that the young girl, who had selflessly tossed an apple to a little Jewish boy, had come to the fence at Schlieben to throw him apples and help sustain him.

As he thought about his past, Herman wove Roma's love into the tapestry of caring that had ensured his survival during the war. He wrote Roma into his story and placed her where she belonged: she was an angel at the fence during his darkest hour, destined to save him. An apparition he encountered long before he met her in the flesh on Coney Island. Yes, he cemented Roma into a corner of his gruesome survivor account and honored her with the love story that she deserved.

When the book was finished, Herman took his efforts to a couple of friends. Can you help me make it better? he asked, and they did. They helped the struggling author correct his poor grammar and untangle the muddled English of his manuscript. Finally, his story was done. Herman felt satisfied and he set it aside.

The door to the Rabbi's office opened again and Herman saw a young man dressed in a business suit, swinging a briefcase, and wearing a yarmulke. Herman looked into his face but the young man was distracted as he exited the Rabbi's sanctuary. Rabbi Oberman smiled at Herman. "Please come in," he said.

Herman felt perfectly comfortable. He trusted the Rabbi. Felt that the man understood what was in his mind. Rabbi Oberman was quite short and slight with narrow shoulders and hips. And a long narrow face with a long straight nose. But in this fine-boned, face were two eyes that were perfectly round and dark, almost like black holes set in the pale skin, eyes that seemed open to everything. Willing to look into another and see all. Soft not penetrating, the Rabbi's eyes promised to try and love everything that they looked into and beheld. Herman was happy to let the Rabbi see him. He had nothing to hide.

Rabbi Oberman spoke first. "Herman why don't you tell me how this whole problem got started," he said. Herman pressed his lips together. He'd been trying to organize it in his head. Where should he start? "You know I told you that after I was shot that my mother came to me in a dream at the hospital and told me to write my story?" he said.

"Yes I remember," the Rabbi said.

"Well I worked very hard. I wrote my shoah account, just like I remembered it. When I couldn't remember things, I talked to Sam. He was older, so he recalled things I couldn't."

"But why the apple, Herman? Why did you write the part about Roma throwing you apples?" The Rabbi spoke gently, keen to get to the heart of it. It wasn't an accusation.

"I told you that I always dreamt about my mother in the camps? I always dreamt that she was coming to me, feeding me. We were starving. The hunger was terrible so we dreamt about food all the time. Mother came to me in my dreams and told me that she would send an angel to watch over me. When I met Roma, after the war, she told me that one time she had thrown an apple to a little Jewish boy and I thought that this could have been me. I wanted it to be me. In my mind, I imagined that the little boy was me and that Roma came to Schlieben and threw the apples to me over the fence."

"Did you discuss this with other people?" the Rabbi asked.

"Not really," Herman said, "maybe a few. But when I wrote the book in 1993, I put it there, because to me it was true."

"So how did people find out about the apple story? How come you wound up on the Oprah show?"

"One day," Herman said, "I think it was in 1995, I was eating lunch and reading the New York Post. They always had these quizzes and contests I liked to look at. One day there was a contest that they asked people how did you meet your wife or husband? The winner would get a Valentine's Day dinner for two."

"So you entered the competition? the Rabbi asked.

"Yes, I wrote that when my wife was a girl during the war in Germany, she came to the concentration camp where I was and threw me apples over the fence to feed me. And then 12 years after the war, after we had both come to America, we met on a blind date and got married."

"Did you think you would win?"

"Not really. But I did and then after that all the newspapers were writing about the story."

"Weren't you uncomfortable because you knew you had imagined the story?

"No. Even though the story wasn't true, it was true to me."

"You know that it is difficult for people to swallow this Herman? That you talked yourself into believing something that you knew wasn't true?" the Rabbi said.

"I know," Herman said." He looked directly at the Rabbi. Didn't shirk his gaze.

"Then what happened?"

"So all the newspapers were writing about it. Lots of headlines and interviews and photographs and some people put it in a book."

"You weren't worried that people would figure out that it wasn't true?" The Rabbi interrupted Herman again.

"No, not really."

"So tell me about the Oprah show," the Rabbi urged.

"One day," Herman said, "one of Oprah's producers called me. She said that she had read about my love story with my wife and she thought it was a very moving story. Very special and she asked me to go on the show."

"What did you say?" The Rabbi leaned forward in his chair and smiled at Herman.

"I said I didn't want to go on the show."

"Now were you concerned that people would find out the story wasn't true?"

"No I didn't really think about that."

"So, why did you finally decide to go on the show?"

"Well, the producer called me a couple more times and I kept telling her no and then one day Oprah called me herself. She said I am personally asking you to come on my show and tell your story."

"Oprah called it the greatest love story ever told," the Rabbi said.

"Yes. The audience liked the story. They were mostly women there and they were crying. The story made them very happy."

"And what did you think about that?"

"I was very happy. My father taught me never to hate, to be tolerant, to be positive. After the Oprah show, I got a lot of letters from people, all different kinds of people. From children and from people who were depressed and said that my story made them feel better and gave them a reason to live." Herman slipped a hand in his jacket pocket and pulled out a letter. "I got this note." He looked at the Rabbi.

"Go ahead and read it," the Rabbi said.

"Dear Mr. Rosenblat," Herman began to read, "I am very angry with my parents because they taught me to hate people. When I hear what happened to you, it makes me feel that I don't want to hate no more." Herman looked at the Rabbi. "It is from a boy called Jose from Queens, New York." Herman folded the letter and tucked it back in his pocket. There was a pause.

"Tell me about the children's book," the Rabbi said.

"A writer did a children's picture book about a girl who saves a little boy by throwing him apples."

"You were becoming famous. Did you enjoy the attention?"

"Oh yes, it was nice. A producer came to me and told me that he wanted to turn the story of the apple into a movie. He said it would be like the movie, 'A Beautiful Life', and later, the other one, 'The Boy in the Striped Pajamas'."

"Have you seen those movies?" the Rabbi asked.

"No I haven't seen them, but somebody sent me a movie poster of 'The Boy in The Striped Pajamas'. It's a little boy sitting at a camp fence wearing the striped pajamas, you know like the uniform we used to wear?" Herman said and the Rabbi nodded.

"Last year, I went on the Oprah show again. Roma and me, we went on for a special Valentine's Day show. I gave Roma a ring to celebrate that we have been married for over 50 years."

"What about your shoah account, Herman? Didn't it bother you that everyone just wanted to talk about the apple and not the things that really happened to you in the Holocaust?"

"Oh sure, it did bother me but the apple story was only a few pages in my book. Everything else is about what happened to my family and me."

"When did you decide to publish your book?"

" A couple of years ago I think. An agent found out that I had written a book. She kept calling me for about six months. She said that publishers were interested in my story. I wasn't sure that I wanted to do it. She kept calling me and I finally said yes. She found a writer to help make the writing better, you know? The book tells about everything that happened to me and to my family. What happened in Wolborz and Piotrkow ghettos; in Buchenwald, Schlieben and Theresienstadt."

"But it was the apple that interested people the most?" It was a bitter pill for the Rabbi and he couldn't hide the look of disappointment that he allowed to cross his face. The annihilation of millions in the camps of Germany; the extermination of six millions Jews, including 80 percent of the finest rabbis and scholars of Talmud and Torah; the devastation of a people and its culture, and the public wanted to read about a dime-store romance?

"Herman," the Rabbi was somber now, "people can forgive you for imagining things that did not happen, but many cannot forgive you for continuing to tell the fiction like it was fact after the people around you told you to stop. Your family, your friends, and the people who knew better told you to stop but you wouldn't." The Rabbi was kind but firm. He had heard the stories that Herman had justified his embellishments because they were entertaining and inspirational to others as though that somehow made them okay.

"But the apple was a hook," Herman said. "People don't want to read about the Holocaust, but the apple drew them to my story, to what happened to me in the Holocaust."

"It's time to stop, Herman." The Rabbi smiled and stood up, the tragic implications of Herman's pronouncement ringing in his heart and in his ears. He held open the door. "Herman, the Holocaust doesn't need any hooks," he said. "No fiction, no matter how captivating, can be allowed to stand in place of the truth. There can be no lies, no distortions, and no denials, only the truth. This is how we honor those who perished and try to make sure that it doesn't happen again. It is not really the fiction, but that you kept repeating the fiction as fact that has hurt your community. This is what you must atone for." The Rabbi squeezed Herman's hand.

"I know," Herman said, and he made his way out into the glare of the Florida sunshine.

Chapter Fifteen
Aftermath

Herman walked his fingers across the books in his bookshelf and pulled out the one he was looking for. It was the finished but unpublished account of his Holocaust experiences, embellished with the story he had imagined of Roma throwing apples to him in Schlieben. Just as he had explained to the Rabbi, this personal fantasy had become the general hook for the book—the reason readers would pick it off the shelves and tell their friends to read it. A book about the Holocaust. Not the greatest tragedy ever told, but apples over a fence—the greatest love story every told. Herman looked at the cover art: a picture of a little girl, an angel at a barbed-wire fence, who had come to toss apples. There were no images that reflected the horror imprinted on Herman's brain for nearly 70 years now: no skeletons in cattle cars, no ovens, no discarded infants with broken skulls. Few people wanted to see these. Not even him. Especially not him.

As the publication date for his memoir neared, Herman had not realized that the window for making an explanation was quickly closing. Soon his story would be set in type, as memoir and as fact. Embellishment that had made sense to him as he pieced together his personal account and fabrications that sugar coated and gave meaning to the horror that he had lived through, were about to be catalogued as all true. Not presented as a story only based on true events. And that was a problem. Just as a teaspoon of sewage added to a barrel of beer creates a barrel of sewage. So, for some, Herman's imaginings about Roma and the apples had contaminated his story—all of it.

As news of the upcoming book spread, Herman saw the trickle of skepticism about his story swell to a torrent. He read the rebuttals that were showing up in print and on the Internet: a girl tossing apples into a concentration camp? It never happened. Could not have happened. Pure fiction. Bad fiction. The fence at Schlieben was heavily patrolled and electrified, no one could get near it. Three sides of the fence were inside a compound and the fourth was next to the guard barracks. The camp was several miles from the town and the road leading to it was guarded. Who could get near? Certainly not a young girl. And how could it have been Roma? Yes, she was passing as a Christian, but her family was living over two hundred miles away from Schlieben.

The gloves were off. The historians, the writers, the PhDs, the bloggers, the commentators, investigators and journalists all came after Herman and his story. His critics were getting louder. What had happened, they said, was that Herman Rosenblat had lied. And why had he lied? For just two reasons: money and fame. And what about those who had helped him? They were enablers and just as guilty. Everyone who rode in Herman's wake--the writers, agents, publishers, producers, journalists and such? They had never even bothered to check the facts.

Herman saw that there was no shading in the attacks. It was black and white. His critics were calling him an immoral liar. His fiction, they said, was doing irreparable harm to the Holocaust cause. It is damaging the legacy of those who were slaughtered, and those who survived, they said. Other survivors had only wanted to tell the truth and be believed. Now the integrity of every account would be called into question. It is a tragedy. It is heartbreaking. And it is all Herman's fault.

Every day, Herman read the swill of commentary, debate and denunciation, and did what he had learned to do in the face of danger: he hunkered down. But the story had touched a nerve and the pressure on him was growing. His phone rang. Sometimes it was someone from his family. "Herman this has gone far enough," they said. "You have to tell the truth about the story. Tell what is real and what's imagined." The agent was calling. The publisher was calling. The movie producer was calling. And everyone's question was the same: did the apple story really happen, Herman?

Herman wanted to explain, but he didn't know how. He lost weight--11 pounds. He worried and could not sleep. He sat for hours at a time in his chair. One night, he had a dream—the one he had told to Rabbi Oberman: he walked into a room and saw Abraham, Isydor, Eva and Sam, dancing together. They were all dead now. Sam had been the last to go just last year. But in his dream, Herman reunited with them all. He looked over and saw Mamusia by the doorway. She was smiling because her family was together and happy. The dream was a good omen, he decided. He let it calm him

But just weeks before the book was due to go on sale, the controversy heated to boiling point and was ready to explode. Herman answered another call from his agent. "Please Herman," she said, "tell me the truth. There is so much evidence to prove that the apple story is not true. So many people want to hear from you. If you made it up, please admit it, explain why you did it, and say you are sorry."

"I always imagined that the story was true. To me, it is true, but it did not really happen." There, Herman had finally said it.

The book was canceled. Tall stacks were left in the warehouse, unshipped to the bookstores that had been expecting them just in time for Valentine's Day. Herman imagined that everyone who had supported him now felt embarrassed and betrayed. Everyone who had attacked him was jubilant at bringing him down.

The press wrote stories with headlines sure to fly: Holocaust Memoir Hoax. Oprah Duped Again by Writer. Something like it had happened before, Herman found out. Oprah had recommended the memoir of a former drug addict. But it turned out that the writer had exaggerated events in his book. People wrote that it was only super-sized stories that seemed to sell these days. But Herman had not set out to dupe Oprah and write a bestselling book.

Herman fretted. He felt sad and sometimes foolish. He was disappointed that his story of hope was now a tool in the hands of cynics and haters. Someone sent him an email and told him that he should have just published his story as a novel. Apparently it was all in how you labeled things. Beneath the defenses he felt forced to assume, Herman understood the outrage. He knew that while he did not see it as a lie or mean it as a lie that his accusers saw his embellishment as just that--a lie. And now they were out for his blood.

But not everyone was against him. Herman stayed home, and each morning, he fired up his computer and tracked the debate raging on the Internet. He discovered that he did have supporters, lots of them. He read their comments on news and blog sites: what difference does it make if some incidents in the book are embellished? It's still a beautiful story. Show me a memoir that isn't inaccurate. Just call it a novel and put it in a different section of the bookstore. Lay off the old man. Who cares?

Friends sent him articles from psychologists. They explained that people, especially children, who had suffered trauma as severe as he had, often reconstructed memories, reshaped the truth and romanticized events to make them bearable. Rabbi Oberman had told him this too, but Herman did not really understand it. He had done what he had done for reasons that made sense to him; reasons that only made his critics more enraged.

The painful denunciations were repeated: hundreds of brave survivors gave scrupulous accounts, but Herman Rosenblat has tarnished his own account and theirs with a lie about his love life. He has sugar-coated what should be left unvarnished as utter, irredeemable and senseless horror. No good came from the Holocaust. No love story. No redemption. It was an evil twisted wasteland in the landscape of humanity. Herman Rosenblat has let the side down and he will not be forgiven. He has hurt his fellow survivors who have suffered enough. And he has given ammunition to the anti-Semites and Holocaust deniers who are having a field day with this debacle.

Sure enough, the anti-Semites were weighing in too: every Jew lies, they said. The Holocaust never happened. Here is just another piece of evidence to prove the Zionist conspiracy. If he lied about the apple, then Rosenblat lied about everything. He is a dirty lying Jew, just like all the rest.

Herman sat at his computer with the photo of Oprah on the wall above it. He scrolled through this ranting and snorted. "Once a Jew hater, always a Jew hater," he said out loud. "They don't need any reason to hate." He thought about the babies in Piotrkow. Their heads smashed against the wall of the synagogue. They had not been old enough to embellish. Not old enough to know that they were Jews even, but they were Jews, and because of this, and only this, they were sentenced to die. Anti-Semitism. Who knew better than he that it was a chronic condition and there was no cure for it?

Herman lay in bed at night and contemplated the historians and PhDs. They study and write books, he thought, they analyze reports of the Holocaust, scrutinize maps, and walk what is left of the camps. They give speeches and attend symposia. They articulate the causes and effects of Nazi terror. They do a fine job of memorializing events. They guard against the actions and attitudes that fuelled the Holocaust so that it will never happen again. And that is good. But.

These learned people, Herman realized, had excellent credentials that he, a boy grown to an old man without the benefit of a real education, did not have. Herman Rosenblat's only Holocaust credential was that he had been there during the dark times that historians now pored over and wrote about. He had lived through every awful minute of it. He had seen his father die from typhus that could have been avoided or treated. He had stood by in terror as his mother had been selected for "processing", for murder. He had worked as a slave for four years in worn out uniforms caked in blood and excrement. He had dragged and tossed bodies into careless heaps and scraped shit out of death trains when he should have been running in fields and studying in school. He had ridden coal hoppers towards yet another nightmare with putrid, stinking corpses in pools of ice water and urine. And worse, he had grown so used to looking on death that even his child's eyes and heart did not blink or skip a beat when they saw it.

At 14, Herman was already 80. The Joy that usually infects youth had not reached him until much later in life. To be sure, Herman thought, he had enjoyed the happiness that his fabled love story had brought him. Reveled in the warmth, affection, and attention that it had won him, but he had not set out to get this for himself. But what was the point of talking? No one was listening. If there was one thing that Herman was schooled enough to know: it was useless trying to explain to those who refused to understand.

Chapter Sixteen
Showtime

"Goodbye dear. Have a good time. Relax and enjoy yourself." Herman gave Roma a kiss and a tense wave, then watched her stroll, a little unsteady on her feet, down the narrow exterior balcony outside their apartment towards the elevator. He had sent his darling wife, all dressed up in cream pants and a pink blouse, and clutching her pocket book by her side, off for the day to visit with a friend. He came inside and closed the screen door of the modest home, the two-bedroom apartment that they had retired to in North Miami Beach.

Today would be too stressful for Roma, Herman had decided. She had not been feeling well. The trembling in her hands was getting worse and the uproar of the last few weeks had made her anxious and depressed. Reporters kept calling and a few had even shown up at the door. Someone had told Herman that this was called door stopping. He called it an ambush and it really scared Roma.

It was now 8 AM and the news crew was due at 9 AM. Herman had spent a good hour the day before on the phone talking to a young producer, Steven, who was coordinating today's shoot at the apartment. "Better there than in-studio," Steven had explained to Herman. "You'll be more relaxed. Don't worry, Herman," he kept repeating on the call, "we are going to make sure we do a piece that is fair." Herman was relieved after he hung up the phone. He felt good about the interview. I want to make my peace, apologize, and explain, he thought. Last night, he had lain in bed tracing the events that had led to this moment. If they just give me a fair hearing, I can explain why I wrote the story the way I did.

When the news crew arrived right at 9 AM, it was already warm out. Herman watched five guys haul heavy black boxes, thick yellow cables, lights on poles, cameras and assorted paraphernalia into the tight space of his small living room. The men in Jeans and T-shirts were polite and cheerful as they moved the furniture around for their set-up. "Don't worry, Mr. Rosenblat, we'll put everything back how we found it," one of them said.

Herman felt energized and caught up in the hum of activity. It was a nice change for a man like him, especially now. He was old, he supposed, but still full of life. The short walks, the trips to the mall, the early-bird dinners, the whiling away of days; sometime it felt like a waste of the energy and vitality he still possessed.

Herman opened the front door to welcome Steven, the producer. In person, he seemed little more than a boy. He was tall and slim with thick dark hair. He had on jeans and a shirt. Polite. Jewish? Yes, Herman was pretty sure that he was. People in television are young, he thought.

Glad of an audience, and eager to share, Herman led the young man to the small bedroom he had converted into a den. He showed him the framed clippings and photos of his beloved family and trusted friends. There, he pointed, was his mother, Rose, and his father, Jacob. There? A family dinner right before the war.

See? He was the young boy near the end. Look at that one. See it? It was the one pride of place--a photograph of Oprah, taken with Herman and Roma, at Harpo Studios in Chicago. He pointed out plaques and certificates. "Not bad for a boy who never went to school?" he said and smiled at the producer, who smiled back as though Herman were a nice Jewish uncle.

The young man humored Herman for at least 15 minutes, trailing the old man from one memento to another, nodding and marking time as the crew worked on the set-up. Herman opened up a folder on his desk. It held a mish mash of photos, articles, remnants from his unique past. Lying there next to a certificate from a North Miami Starbucks, pronouncing Herman Rosenblat "Customer of The Week", the producer saw a black and white photo of skeletal concentration camp survivors. Like living dead, they stared up at him. The producer glanced at another photograph of skeletons, but these were dead, their bodies stacked up outside a barracks building.

"These are men," Herman said, "who died just before or just after the Allies liberated Buchenwald in 1945. They managed to stay alive for so long and then they died right at the last minute." Herman riffled through the papers, though the sacred and profane, the diabolical and mundane. It was all mixed together in his green manila folder, secured with an oversized black paperclip.

Herman heard the screen door. "Oh that's probably Doug, the executive producer," Steven said. "Let me introduce you." Herman shook hands with the head honcho who looked neat in a crisp pink shirt and jeans. He was smaller than Steven and didn't look much older. People in television are young, Herman thought again. This new guy was all business. Herman asked if he wanted to see his photographs, but Doug just waved him off. He got right to it, to the important work of producing: setting up a feed, experimenting with the seating and the lighting. Then fifteen minutes before they were due to begin, Herman noticed another player walk in.

"This is our correspondent, Andy," Steven said. Andy held out his hand for a quick shake and Herman felt the subtle brush-off. Steven had told Herman that he might recognize Andy, because, "He reads the news for one of the big three networks sometimes." Herman studied his face but it didn't ring a bell. Andy was all dressed up in a suit and tie and he wore makeup. Herman noticed it during their lightening-fast handshake. It made him look pale, like he wasn't feeling well.

"Herman, can you come over and sit on this chair please?" No-nonsense Doug was gesturing with a cupped hand like he wanted to scoop Herman into one of his own straight-backed white dining room chairs.

"You don't want me on the sofa?" Herman glanced over at the comfortable spot in the living room.

"Nah too soft," Doug said. "You'll sink into it and it won't look right on television."

Herman gingerly stepped over the cables and took his seat on the dining chair under a small forest of tripod lights. A soundman clipped a microphone to his lapel and lifted his jacket so he could tuck the little package attached to the mic into the waistband of his pants. Herman had dressed up in a suit, shirt and tie. His eyesight was very bad, so he wore his eyeglasses with lenses like fish-bowl glass that made his eyes look giant.

"Can you take your glasses off, Mr. Rosenblat?" Doug called from the kitchen where he had set up his monitor to monitor Herman. Herman took his glasses off. He wasn't sure where the camera was; where he should look. There was a pause and then Doug spoke. "Put 'em back on, please." Another pause. "No, take 'em off." Pause. "Yeah, just go ahead and keep 'em off please, Mr. Rosenblat." Herman put the spectacles in his top pocket. The dark under-eye shadows and sagging skin were visible now and his eyesight was dimmer. Without magnification, his eyes looked smaller and less alert. He rubbed them, the way old people often do, like a tired child. He squinted and looked vulnerable. Like a worried soul struggling to bring his world into focus.

Now Andy sat down opposite Herman. He was avoiding eye contact. Making no effort to put Herman at his ease the way they usually did before a television interview. Herman had done quite a few after all and he knew. "Ready?" Andy flicked his eyes at Herman. Herman nodded. He thought he did feel ready. He was clear, but a little nervous now. Herman didn't know what was going to happen, but he could feel the current. It all felt too businesslike.

Andy got straight to it. He directed Herman to watch a small TV monitor, then he played the tape of Herman's second appearance on Oprah, the Valentine's Day one. Herman saw himself. There he was on one knee, presenting his ring to Roma, claiming his undying love. Why not? Fifty years of marriage is a long time. As he watched, nothing on Herman's face registered that he realized how the scene might look to others; that it might seem unpalatable given the recent developments.

The tape revealed the mood on Oprah's stage that day--festive and exuberant. There were tight shots of women in the audience. They were happy and moved, carried away by the scene playing out on the stage. By contrast, right now in the clutter and tension of his small apartment, Herman could feel the strain. They had just started and it already felt like a brightly lit interrogation room. The soundmen and camera crew looked busy and absorbed by their tasks. Was Herman imagining it or did they seem a bit uncomfortable as they watched the interviewer wind up to grill an old man as he sat captive and upright on his own slightly grubby dining room chair, not quite knowing what to expect?

Right off the bat, the reporter's questions sounded like accusations to Herman. Not so much the words as the tone. They came at him in quick succession like arrows at a target: "What do you think when you watch this tape of your performance on Oprah?"

"What do you say to the people you have hurt?"

"Your brother turned away from you on his deathbed, didn't he?"

"Your lies have hurt your son. Let me read you something he said…"

Herman listened and tried to keep up with the litany of condemnation. He had rehearsed his explanations in his head. But this wasn't the calm of his bedroom where he mulled things over in the dark as Roma lay sleeping beside him.

Herman's stress level was going up and his clarity was coming down. He couldn't formulate a proper answer to the questions that were blowing up around him like grenades. He was coming unstitched, wrestling with his second language, English. Faltering and failing to express himself clearly. He tried to focus on the interviewer and his long list of questions but he found himself dragged away by an inner dialogue. Why are they attacking me with my family? Isn't there history in every family? Complex and confusing dynamics that make relationships un-mapable to everyone except the people who are in them? Why are they using my own flesh and blood to indict me? Yes there is conflict, but not alienation? Dirty laundry on national television, just to make a point?

The allegations about his brother really hurt. Sam had certainly not turned away from him on his deathbed. Herman had read this lie in blogs and news stories. It hurt him where other untruths missed. He had gone almost every day to visit Sam while he was sick. And Sam had said that he liked his book. Everything except the apple. Sam had looked at Herman, shook his head, and given him a look. Irritation not anger. There had been no deathbed denouncement of Herman by Sam. Had they come through hell to be splintered by something like this? Those years in the camps, there had been four Rosenblat brothers. Where one goes, we all go. They had stuck together until the end. But today, Herman was alone.

"That is not true," Herman said to the interviewer. "My brother did not turn away from me." The correspondent looked down at his notes. He had more. "Where is your wife?" he asked.

"She has gone out for the day," Herman said.

"Why isn't Roma here today?"

"Because, she is not well and all of this," Herman gestured to take in all the commotion in the room and the stress he felt in his gut, "is too much for her."

"Why did your wife lie for you?" the correspondent asked. There was something painful in the way that Andy put Roma and the word lie in the same sentence. Herman was tough. How could he not be? He had lived through the ultimate boot camp. He thought about Roma. Always a little fragile. The price she was paying now. It scraped his underbelly. "Because she loves me," Herman said and repeated it to be clear. "Because she loves me."

"You had a real Holocaust story. Why did you make up the story of the apple?" Andy asked now. Herman was still stinging from the last question. He tensed up and spit out his answer. "My wife told me that when she was a girl she threw an apple to a Jewish boy. I imagined that boy was me. In my mind, I still believe it is me," Herman said, repeating the answer that all of his critics asked for but none of them believed.

"If you had to do it all over again, would you tell the story in the same way?" Andy asked and then waited. Anyone watching might have said that Herman did not read the room. He could have said that he was sorry. He could have said I would do things differently if I had to do them over again, but instead, Herman defaulted to what was true for him. He put his head into the carefully tied noose. "Yes, I would do it again," he said. "In my mind, I imagined that the story was true. I still believe it is true." Herman repeated his crazy logic and watched as it put a deep crease on the reporter's carefully powdered and shine-free brow.

"The story of the apple is a hook," Herman went on with his tin ear and his determination to tighten the noose around his neck. "People who don't like to read about the Holocaust wanted to read about my story, because of the apple."

"You can't have it both ways," the reported sneered. "Either you imagined it was true or you made up the apple story to manipulate your readers. To hook them like you say."

No, Herman thought, that's not what he had meant. Why were people better than he was at stating their version of his story? What he had meant to say, but couldn't, was that he had knit an imagined apple into the fabric of his story; decided that it belonged and left it there. Like when you plaster over a hole in the wall. You can see the patch. See that it wasn't always there, but now it is part of the wall; inseparable from the wall. It serves a purpose. The apple made his story whole, gave it the meaning he needed. It made him feel better. It made the people who heard about it feel better. It belonged. The apple had power. It caught people with its message. It was a happy accident, an unexpected windfall. It proved that his instinct and his need to romanticize his own agony had been correct.

"I think we're finished," the reporter said. He looked at a

cameraman and twirled his finger. A TV sign. "Thank you, Mr. Rosenblat." He stood up, shook Herman's hand, lightening fast again, and then turned away to more important business.

"We have to hotfoot it back to New York," Doug, the senior producer, told Herman as he inserted important papers into his messenger bag. "We've scheduled a late-night editing session to make sure the piece will be ready for an early-morning broadcast." Doug stuck one arm through the messenger bag and pulled it over his head.

Herman listened to Doug's last-minute directions to the crew. Get the B-roll. Put everything back in order. Herman carried two dirty coffee cups into the kitchen and turned around just in time to see the two men--the important producer, and the interviewer with the make-up, dart out like two cowboys blowing out of Dodge.

The freelance cameramen still had work to do. They asked for a few more shots: you in your den looking at photos, Mr. Rosenblat. You in your kitchen making coffee. You outside looking off into the distance. If he had known how to stop and register it, Herman would have felt the careful crafting of the story around him. As it was, he didn't know that the tape would be putty in the producers' hands as they sculpted just the right caricature of Herman that they were looking for.

Herman had known only friendly not punitive TV. He did not know "chew em up, cram them in a news cycle, then spit them out" TV. He had been spoiled by Oprah and her "guest accommodations provided by a fancy hotel with a tiled bathroom as big as his den" brand of television. It was better.

Herman didn't know that for the last few days, his critics had been busy briefing the producer. They had given him quite an earful. And all through the interview, they had been busy on the sidelines, monitoring the proceedings and texting play-by-play directions. Nail him with this fact. Skewer him with this quote. Ask about this outrage or that lie. The producer had already bought their angle. He had picked a team and landed on the side of seeming propriety and conventional wisdom. He would try to be balanced, but really, shouldn't Herman Rosenblat's fantasy about his Holocaust love story result in its surgical dissection and a kind of public flogging?

Herman got up the next morning. He encouraged Roma to sleep in a little while longer. He did not want her to see the interview and be upset. Right before 7 AM, he brought his morning coffee into the living room, sat on the cream leather couch, switched on the television and caught the teasers for his upcoming interview on the morning news show: "An exclusive: the man behind the Holocaust memoir hoax speaks out." Later, another one: "Coming up, an interview with the man who lied to Oprah."

Some time before 8 AM, the interview finally aired. It lasted three maybe four minutes. Herman watched and thought the whole thing was fairly unremarkable--a let down. His big moment to explain and apologize had fizzled and died. The reporter sounded snarky; his contempt leaking out during the cut-away shots. As for his own performance, Herman could see as he watched himself that the piece exposed what he had been feeling--plenty befuddled and grumpy. He noticed that he often sounded confused, thwarted, and unable to express himself. As the piece finished, the older but attractive blond anchor came on. She was skilled at television transitions. She pronounced herself "mystified" by Herman's explanation, shaking her head in a hammy TV-style double take, and then she said, "Next up."

Right away the phone rang. "Herman, stop being a dummy." It was Harry, Herman's good friend and exasperated lawyer. He had seen the show. "Keep quiet now," he said. "What good can come from talking to these people in the media? They don't care. It's all just ratings to them. You can't explain this. They don't want to hear it. People are out for your blood. Just stay schtum, Herman." Then Harry hung up.

Maybe Harry was right. It was impossible to pack the method and madness of almost 80 years of tumultuous life into a four-minute interview. Out of nowhere, a feeling of despair washed over Herman. Only now and then since the war years had he felt like giving up. Really, after everything, what could be so bad? But today felt like one of those days. Herman tried to fall back on an old trick, a thought that had dominated life in the camps: what will be will be.

He felt suddenly tired. He went to lie down. Roma was up now. He could hear her in the bathroom. The bright Florida light had a golden note as it filled the bedroom and lit the flowered cover on his and Roma's queen-sized bed. Herman stretched out on it and closed his eyes. Unleashing his strained and tethered mind, he let his thoughts roam.

How often in the last few weeks had he seen his name written with the word liar next to it? Lies, lies, lies. How many times during the war had a lie been his friend and savior? What was a lie? On the road to Warsaw with his family all those years ago when they needed food and shelter: "Are you a Jew?" the innkeeper had asked.

"No we are not Jews?" Herman and his father had answered.

"Herman, tell them your are 16," Isydor had ordered as he pushed him towards the SS officer for selection. He wanted to guarantee him a slot with the men selected for work. Was trying to spare his little brother a spot in the mounting piles of the old, sick, young and weak, who were marked for extermination.

"I don't love you, Herman. Get over there with your broth-